DEMON SEEKERS
The Journey Begins

Written by
June Lundgren

Table of Contents

The Arrival 3
The Partnership 20
The Journey Begins 40
A Message from Azuriel........48
Lucifer Interferes.................60
Angelic Rescue...................67
Sara's Arrival....................80
Lebanon demon.................91
Sanctuary.........................99
A Cry for Help..................113
The Trap.........................117
Making the Connection.........122
Battle Against Evil..............132
About the Author...............142

The Arrival

It seemed to Gabe that the night was unusually quiet, he had never felt an evening quite like this. It was as if the world were waiting for some great event to occur. Automatically he slowed his car down as if something were telling him to be careful. He drove for another quarter of a mile until he saw a large imposing silhouette against the night sky. His eyes strained to make out details of what was left of the structure. By the outline of the architecture, he could tell that it was a church at one time and it may have been Presbyterian. It looked like it had been abandoned long ago. He found an overgrown driveway that seemed to lead straight towards the church. Pulling carefully off of the road, he turned his SUV down the driveway.

The driveway stretched on for about half a mile, then suddenly the ruins of the church appeared before him. Pulling up as close as he could to the church, he turned off the car and sat for a moment just staring at what was left of it. He had the oddest feeling as if he were always meant to be here. He could hear the crickets playing their music and an owl hooting nearby. It was the perfect summer evening, clear and warm.

All of his life he had been having dreams of this particular church. The dream is what got him interested in the paranormal which in turn led him to become an avid writer of paranormal mysteries. Ever since he could remember, he had had paranormal experiences. He had joined a local paranormal investigative group when he first bought his ranch ten years ago. During the last twenty years, he had seen more types of entities than most investigators do in a lifetime. The other members of his paranormal group called him a ghost magnet.

He never knew the name of the church in the dream, but it was always the same. In the dream, he was standing facing the ruins of the church. But he didn't look like a human. Instead, he was an angel with pure white wings and a golden countenance.

Another much larger angel appeared to him. The angel pointed towards what was left of the door and said: "Enter, your journey has just begun and your guide awaits you." He got the impression that it was important for him to go inside. The dream always ended the same way, with his pushing open the heavy wooden door.

He had spent most of his adult life searching for the church in his dream. He had learned from his research that the church in his dream was Presbyterian because of its architecture. They all seemed to have high formidable looking spires. He spent hours on the internet investigating every possible lead on abandoned churches. Now that he was here looking at the building he knew it was the one from his dreams. Glancing at his watch, he was surprised to see that it had only taken him an hour and a half to get here.

Taking a deep breath, he grabbed his flashlight and the bag of equipment out of the car. He always carried his equipment for paranormal investigating with him wherever he went searching for the church. Turning on the flashlight, he made his way to the large imposing wooden doors at the top of the steps. He examined the structure and condition of the door to make sure that it hadn't rotted and was stable enough to be opened. Finding very little in the way of wood rot, he checked the rot iron hinges and pulled on the handles. They seemed to be a little rusty, nothing more. Just as he was just reaching out his hand to grab the door handle, it started to open slowly.

Having investigated the paranormal for many years, he was accustomed to the unexplained, but usually, it was proceeded by a cold spot, sound, smell or sense of dread. This time there was nothing. He couldn't shake the feeling that something important was about to happen. Calming his mind and opening his senses he reached out to see if he could get an awareness of whatever had opened the door. It was then that he noticed the night had gone strangely silent.

Holding very still, he listened for any noise or movement around him. The wind that just a few moments ago had been rustling through the trees had stopped. The crickets and owl he heard while sitting in the car were silent. If he didn't know any better, he could swear he was caught in a single moment in time.

Just as the thought occurred to him, he dismissed it as fantasy. Looking down at his watch, he was shocked to find that the sweeping second hand had stopped. He tapped the face of the watch thinking maybe the second hand was just stuck. It was then he noticed the time on his watch was the same as it had been when he arrived. He had heard of people experiencing time loss during investigations, but he had never heard of time stopping. A jolt of fear shot through him. A sudden chill encompassed his body and the hairs on his arms, and the back of his neck was standing on edge. He knew with every fiber of his being that there was something waiting inside for him.

Just what it was he couldn't say for sure, but he was praying it wasn't something negative.

Taking a deep breath, he slowly pushed the door the rest of the way open. Stepping into the building, he noticed that same sense of timelessness he had experienced outside. The inside of the church was empty. Plants had begun to creep through the stone cracks in the floor and walls. He could only surmise that the wooden pews that used to fill the room were removed long ago. His footsteps echoed eerily as he made his way towards what use to be the pulpit. He sat his bag down on the stone altar.

Opening up the bag, he pulled out his EMF (electromagnetic frequency) detector, camcorder, digital recorder, and headphones. He sat the camera on the alter and positioned it, so it covered the entire room. He plugged his headphones into the recorder and turned it on. Turning on the EMF detector, he sat it next to his bag on the altar. Stepping down from altar he made his way to the center of the room. He stood there for several minutes, but the only sound he could hear was the sound of his heartbeat. He was about to give up when the air around him changed dramatically. He froze straining to see or hear anything, anything at all.

Then he heard it, a soft whisper of a voice through the recorder say, "She's coming."

"Who's coming?" He wondered.

"She's coming; she's coming, you'll see!" Another voice responded.

He heard a male voice say, "She's coming, learn well."

"Who's coming and what am I supposed to learn?" he asked out loud. "Why won't you tell me who's coming?" he paused waiting for a reply

"The warrior is coming, and the journey begins." Whispered a voice in his ear that sent shivers down his spine. "Your destiny is revealed."

"What do you mean it's my destiny? Are you talking about the dreams?" he asked

All through the exchange, the EMF detector hadn't alarmed once which was extremely odd. He had never known it not to alarm in the presence of a ghost or negatives. He knew there were new batteries in the device because he had checked them before he left the house. Heading back to where the meter sat he picked it up and checked the battery level which was at full strength. He pushed the test button, and it tested fine. Well if the voices weren't ghosts or negatives just what were they? This was the first time in twenty years of investigating that this had ever happened.

Suddenly the atmosphere in the church changed dramatically. The room felt electrically charged and heavy at the same time. He took a moment to analyze what he was feeling. He wasn't sure why he was feeling a heaviness in his chest, it was as if he couldn't get a full breath. The shift in the church was palpable as if even the night air was holding its breath waiting for something of great importance to occur.

For the first time, he was questioning his decision to enter the building. The voice had said it was his destiny and the only thing he could think of was the dream. It had to have some connection; there was no other logical explanation he could think of.

Checking his recorder, he realized to his dismay that the batteries were dead. He headed to where his bag sat on the alter and dug out some new batteries. He finished installing the new batteries and turned on the recorder. Turning back to face the center of the room he held out his recorder hoping to get some answers.

"If you're not a ghost and you're not a demon what are you?" he asked not sure if he wanted to know the answer.

His question was met with silence at first then his question was answered in a way that he would never have expected in a million years.

What sounded like a loud clap of thunder echoed around the room and a flash of light so bright that it rivaled the sun filled the room for a moment. The light blinded him for a moment, and when his vision cleared, he couldn't believe his eyes. There in the center of the room, a figure which was unmistakably female knelt on one knee; arms braced on the cold stone floor. He couldn't see her face because her long black hair hung down over her it. He stood frozen in place staring at the figure.

He unconsciously gasped in surprise, but it wasn't the fact the being was female that made him gasp. It was the sight of what was protruding out of her back. Protruding from her shoulder blade area was a pair of large whitish-silver wings folded close against her body. By his estimate, her wings would have a nearly eleven-foot span. Her long, black hair was thick from what he could see of it. He had been so busy obsessing about her wings that he hadn't realized her head was up and she was looking directly at him.

Their eyes met, and he was startled by their clarity and color. Her eyes were such a light color of pale green as if to be almost white. He suddenly realized that she was talking to him, but her lips were not moving. He thought to himself it must be a form of telepathy only he couldn't understand the language she was speaking at first. After a sentence or two, the words started making sense to him as if she had suddenly switched from her language to English.

He responded to her the same way that she had communicated with him, telepathically.

"Who are you? What are you? Are you an angel?" He fired the questions at her rapidly.

"Humans, you always have to complicate everything." She commented standing up and turning to face him. For the first time, he noticed that she wore a white robe of some kind.

Reading his thoughts, she told him, "This garment you see is out of difference to the human condition."

"What do mean human condition?" He asked his eyes and thoughts returning to her wings.

"You mortals wear clothing to cover your bodies; we have no such trappings on the other side. The appendages that you see as wings are nothing more than white light energy. They provide stabilization, protection and act as a shield. We use our wings, as you call them, to shield us if we do not wish to be detected like when we are in the presence of a demon."

As he watched, he saw her wings slowly fade into nothingness. Now there was nothing to indicate that she was anything other than a mortal woman.

"You never answered my question. You're obviously not a demon or an earthbound spirit so that only leaves one thing; you must be an angel. But I would wager no ordinary angel, maybe an archangel like Michael."

"Very good Gabe, Michael said you are intelligent for a mortal. My soul name is Sayetta, and I am an avenging Angel. I dispense retribution that is so ordered by the creator. Although not as well-known as the others I am sent out when things need a hands-on approach."

"Okay, so why are you here and why have you taken on human form? I've heard of instances where people have been in the presence of angels, and they look and act like humans, but they're never here for very long. They always have a purpose so what is your purpose? And what do I have to do with all of this?"

"All valid questions, let's go outside." She said heading for the door.

He followed her out the large wooden door. She had taken a seat on the top step, and he sat down beside her. As he sat down, he felt the cold from the stone penetrate his jeans.

"I am the one who gave you the dream about this place."

"Okay, but why so early in my life, I've experienced this dream repeatedly all my life. Couldn't you have waited until I was an adult?"

"To you, it was years to us on the other side it was but a moment ago; I purposely made it repeat every year on the same date. I did this so that you would remember and search for the building."

"Oh, I remembered alright, it became an obsession that almost drove me crazy. So, what you're telling me is I'm supposed to be here at this exact time to meet you. But why me, what's so special about me? I'm just an ordinary guy."

She stared at him for the longest time. Just when he was sure she wasn't going to answer, she started speaking.

"Your soul belongs to a warrior angel. We have worked together in your other lives. You reincarnate in each life to work with me to fight the dark ones. You're given certain abilities that enable you to help me seek out and find the demons. You help me, and I help you learn to use your abilities to find demons and send them back where they belong."

"It sounds like a good partnership, but I don't know how to find them, and even if I did find them, I'm only human. Doesn't it take divine intervention to remove them? I've seen priests performing exorcisms, and it always seems to take an inordinate amount of time for them to remove the demon. If it takes priests days, weeks or even months to remove them, how could I possibly do it? I'm not a holy man nor do I profess to be a demonologist."

"That's true you're not a holy man. Have you never wondered why it takes these holy men so long to remove a demon?" She asked him.

"No, not really. I guess I always thought you had to wear down the negative before it would release its hold on a person."

"Doubt, fear and lack of faith are the enemy when it comes to dealing with the dark ones. The person removing the demon cannot have even the slightest doubt in themselves or their ability to remove the demon. If they have any doubt in themselves or the creator, the negatives zero in on this and will use these weaknesses to their advantage. It will be ten times harder to remove the demon if they can remove it at all."

"Well if priests have doubts, a regular guy like me doesn't stand a snowball's chance in hell." He said.

"Certainly, a colorful and apt metaphor, but not entirely accurate. You believe just because the person studied theology and became a priest it automatically means that they have no doubts or fears about the creator or themselves. This is simply not true, they are just as flawed, and you are. Remember when you were a child and your mother would help you to lay out a snack for Santa and his reindeer? You wanted to believe in him so much you convinced yourself he was real. You had this little tiny doubt in the back of your mind that he wasn't real otherwise, why would you have tried to stay up year after year to get a peek at him."

"I see where you're going with this. Alright, the priests are subject to doubt and fear just like the rest of us when dealing with the dark side. So how does someone like me face and remove one of them?" he asked seriously.

"With a little help from an archangel and a lot of training. Sun Tzu once said, 'know your enemy and know yourself' and Winston Churchill said, 'The only thing you have to fear is fear itself.' Although they were talking about war, this is still sound advice. We are in a spiritual war for the souls of humanity, and it is a war we must not lose."

"I agree and understand. So, your job is to train me to find demons and remove them here in the physical world. What happens once you finish training me?"

"This is something you do not learn overnight its different for every person. It is a process that starts with faith and ends with a strong will. For you, it also means you have to make contact with your angelic soul. The first step is having faith in the creator. The second is learning to have faith in yourself. Your faith in the creator is strong already, but faith in yourself is a bit lacking right now, but we'll fix that." She said grinning at him in a peculiar way.

"I don't think I like the look on your face when you said that." He told her, not sure what to make of it.

She burst out laughing and the stillness that had surrounded him since he arrived suddenly vanished. It was as if her joyous laughter brought the night to life again. "You mortals always have to make things more difficult than they are." She stood up and held out her hands to him. "Come, take my hands, I am going to open you up to the world beyond the physical one you see now."

He got up and placed his hands in her outstretched ones. The moment they made contact he felt a strong electrical-like current pass into his body. Reflexively he tried to snatch his hands away but was unable to break the hold she had on him. She was incredibly strong for such a fragile looking person. After the initial shock, he felt a warmth and sense of peace start to fill him. They stood there for what seemed like hours but in reality, only a few minutes had passed. She released his hands, and he suddenly felt dizzy and disoriented. Once the feeling passed, he felt somehow lighter.

"Close your eyes, open your mind and reach out your senses." She instructed him.

He closed his eyes and listened to the night. He could hear the wind in the trees, crickets chirping and even the sound of his heartbeat.

"I didn't tell you to open your ears; I said open your mind." She scolded him.

"I'm trying, but it's not easy after what I just witnessed."

"You did it when you entered the church." She reminded him.

"Yeah, I know that was before you shattered everything I've ever learned about the paranormal."

"I'm sorry, but you need to know the whole truth, not the half-truths you've learned in the mortal world. Now, imagine that you are in a movie theater and you are surrounded by stark white walls. The only sound in the room is your heartbeat. You can feel and hear the pumping of your heart as the blood is coursing through your veins. Now focus on your heart, gradually slow its beat, yes, that's it. As your heart slows your mind expands and as it expands you are aware of other souls surrounding you, communicating with you. What color are the souls you are seeing?" she asked him.

He could see souls surrounding him just out of reach. *"I wish they would come closer so I could see them better."* He thought to himself. As if in response to his thought the souls reacted by moving closer to him. The closer they got to him the clearer they became. He noticed that most of the souls were pure white, but there were a couple of blue ones mixed between the many white ones. "Most of them are white, but there are a couple of blue ones. There are two really bright blue ones standing in front of me." He told her.

"Open your eyes." She instructed him.

As he opened his eyes, he was struck silent by what he was seeing. He noticed a blue glow emanating from her and standing next to her was the biggest angel he had ever seen. It must have stood a good seven or eight feet tall, and like her, it had a wingspan of at least twelve feet. It was a magnificent sight to behold, and if he was not mistaken, it was a male.

"Right again, I told Sayetta you were a quick study." He confirmed his thoughts telepathically. "I am Michael, the Archangel I oversee all the angels. Your name suits you, Gabe; you are much like your namesake Gabriel."

"You're right as usual Michael he does possess many of Gabe's traits. But does he have the courage to face a demon head on? Only time will tell."

Michael nodded in agreement. "I have some news for you," he said turning to her and talking out loud for the first time. "The first Archangel you seek is in Oregon, and she has learned her true identity. After much self-searching, she has begun to do removals."

Turning to Gabe, he went on to explain. "Each incarnation of an archangel is different, and it is not always easy for the physical consciousness to accept who and what they are. Some of them go insane because the power of what is inside them completely overwhelms them. It has not been easy for this particular one. The person who was to train her crossed before the training was complete. We underestimated the time the physical consciousness needed to prepare for the transition. It is very difficult for us to understand the concept of time as it does not exist where we are."

"Yes, I can see where it could be very overwhelming. Just what's happening here is overwhelming for me." Gabe agreed.

"You'll manage, you always do whenever you incarnate and work with Sayetta. I must go now." Looking at Sayetta, he told her telepathically, *"You must begin his training soon, there is no time to delay. And you must make him understand who and what he is."*

"I understand, I think it's too early to reveal to him the full extent of his identity. I will know when the time is right."

"I recommend that you do it now, the longer the delay, the more dangerous it is for him."

"I will do as you suggest, you have more experience with mortals than I do."

Gabe watched the silent exchange between the two wishing he could hear what was being said. As quickly as he had appeared Michael vanished.

"There is one more detail that needs to be taken care of. Michael urged me to tell you the rest of your story."

"What does he mean by that?"

"Do you remember when Michael said 'whenever you incarnate and work with Sayetta'?" she asked him.

"I remember him saying something to that effect but didn't understand it."

"What he was trying to say is that you also have the soul of a warrior angel. Each time I am sent back into the physical world to do a job for the creator you are born ahead of time to establish yourself in the physical world and await my arrival."

"Holy cow, so I have an angelic soul inside me. Is that why I've always been able to tell where the negatives are whenever I go on an investigation or enter a location?"

"Yes, now I need to awaken the soul consciousness so that he can help us on this quest. I have a feeling that you are going to be one of those who handles the transition well. Are you ready?" she asked him.

He had the feeling whether he was ready or not this waking was about to happen, he just hoped she was right, and he could handle it. Otherwise, he was going to be a basket case.

"Not really but here goes."

She placed one hand on the back of his head and one hand on the top of his head. "Close your eyes and open your mind." She told him.

Just before he closed his eyes, he noticed her physical body melt away and the angelic being that was her true self appear.

He could feel his mind slipping away and a stronger consciousness coming forward. It was like he was watching it happen from a distance. He could see and hear everything that was occurring. His physical body seemed to be changing subtly.

"It's alright Gabe there's nothing be afraid of. Your soul name is Zebulon."

"It just feels strange."

"You will now be able to call on Zebulon whenever you need help or want validation on something," Sayetta informed him removing her hands from him.

Opening his eyes, he noticed she was back to physical form. He felt dizzy, fuzzy headed and shaky. He couldn't shake the feeling that he would never be quite the same again.

"Don't worry, the after effects will pass quickly." She told him.

"I hope so," he said shaking his head trying to clear it.

"We need to leave as soon as possible for Oregon."

"Oregon, why are we going to Oregon?" He wanted to know. "You never did tell me what your actual mission is." He reminded her.

"I'll tell you once we are on our way to your place."

"Alright, I just have to gather up a few things, and then we can go." Heading back inside, he picked up his equipment and returned to where she waited outside. He used his key to open the back of the SUV and placed his equipment inside. Closing the hatch, he motioned for her to get into the passenger seat but she just stared at him. It was then it occurred to him, he had forgotten to unlock the door. "Sorry." He mumbled.

He used his remote to unlock the doors, and they both climbed inside. He wasn't sure what she knew or didn't know about living in the physical world. "You need to wear a seatbelt," he told her, "It goes on like this." He said showing her how it was done. In one fluid movement, she had the seatbelt fixed in place. *She's a quick learner.*" He thought to himself.

"Thank you." She responded.

The Partnership

Starting the car, he turned it back in the direction in which he had come. They had been traveling for several miles, and he wondered if she had forgotten he had asked about her mission. Suddenly she started to speak.

"My 'mission' as your call it, is to find all eight archangels that have been born into the physical world. I need to awaken them to who and what they are. I will also help them integrate their soul consciousness into their physical consciousness like I did with you."

"Why does it have to be integrated? Isn't this something they can do on their own?"

"If the soul consciousness isn't integrated then the physical body will be vulnerable to the dark ones. Once they understand who and what they are, they will be able to defend themselves from the darkness. Their angelic soul will help them sense, see, hear and remove the negatives."

Gabe spent the next couple of hours mulling over the information she had just imparted to him.

They traveled straight through only stopping to get gas and something to drink. Finally, they arrived back at his home outside of Sedona. An electronic gate marked the entry to his property, using his cell phone he entered the gate code, and it slowly opened. The driveway was a quarter mile long lined on either side by fig trees. Arriving at the house, he entered the security code on his phone to turn off the alarm. He activated the garage door remote, and it slowly opened, and he pulled the car inside. Once inside he pushed the remote again, and the door slid closed. Taking off his seat belt, he noticed Sayetta had already removed her's. Getting out of the car, he made his way to the back hatch and gathered his gear. Closing the hatch, he could hear his dog whining inside the house. Heading towards the door leading to the inside of the house, he opened the door. A cold, wet nose greeted him as he pushed it open. Sayetta followed closely behind him, and he was shocked to find his overly protective Pitbull pushing past him to lick and nuzzle her hand.

Usually, Titus never left his side; he was very protective of him and his home. But here he was licking Sayetta's hand and looking up at her adoringly. He should have known Titus would know what she was as animals were more sensitive to the other side. "I can see you've already met Titus." He said with a knowing grin.

"Yes, we have met before in other lifetimes, and he knows me well. As you say, animals are more sensitive to us." She said petting the big dog.

"You'll have to refrain from calling us humans or mortals that's a dead giveaway to anyone listening. Do you have to eat or drink in this form?"

She tilted her head and thought for a moment, "Yes, the physical body requires sustenance as well as sleep. It's always difficult for me to remember what the physical body requires, that is why you are always reborn to await my arrival. I need someone to help me acclimatize to the physical world." Suddenly she was interrupted by the sound of her stomach growling. She looked at him for guidance.

"That is the sound of an empty stomach; you will need to eat and drink something soon. I seem to remember that you should have only plant food, no animal derived food. Are you allowed to drink milk or eat eggs?" He told her his brow furrowed in concentration.

"Yes, that's right, no meat but milk and eggs are acceptable because they are given freely by the animals as gifts to mankind." She said smiling at him.

"Okay let me get my equipment put up then I'll make us a salad for lunch. Why don't you go into the living room and rest while I get things going? Titus will keep you company, won't you boy?" Titus whimpered in agreement and sat down next to Sayetta.

Heading into office, he unpacked his equipment bag and pulled the memory cards out of the equipment and turned on his computer. Once the computer was up and running, he downloaded the discs onto the hard drive. There were no sounds coming from the living room, so he tiptoed to the living room to see what was happening. Sayetta appeared to be asleep on the sofa with Titus laying on the floor beside her. He tiptoed back into his office and sat back to watch the camera footage.

An hour later after reviewing the footage, he was shocked. Nothing, absolutely nothing of was recorded on the footage. He could see himself and his reaction but nothing of Sayetta. Then he turned his attention to the audio files. Listening, he couldn't hear any other voices but his own.

Running his hand through his hair in frustration, he suddenly remembered something his Grandma Ruth had once told him. She told him that angelic beings could not be captured on a camera, it was forbidden for them to show themselves on film.

He had never really believed her before today; now he was forced to believe her.

"I knew you didn't believe me, but I always knew someday you would. You always had to find things out for yourself, never satisfied until you had experienced it for yourself."

Startled he turned around and there before him was the image of his grandmother smiling at him. He blinked several times as if to clear his sight.

"Grandma, is that you?"

"Of course, it's me, who did you think it was. And no I am not a ghost, I am a spirit being."

"I've never seen you in spirit form or an angelic being before today, two firsts, it must be my lucky day. How come I've never see you before?"

"Oh, I've been here, I was assigned as one of your guides after I crossed. Sayetta opened you up that's why you can see me now. But remember you must take the bad with the good. I'll be here to watch your back as I have in all your lives. We've been together a long time you and me."

"This is just too much to take in all at once; I think I need a break." He said watching his grandmother faded into nothingness. "That's it I need a change of venue." He got up and made his way into the kitchen to start making dinner.

In the living room, the woman smiled secretively to herself enjoying his frustration. She felt an odd sensation in her lower abdominal region and wondered what it was. Getting up, she made her way into the kitchen.

He was taking the ingredients out of the refrigerator for a salad when Sayetta walked in and sat down at the kitchen table with Titus close on her heals.

Gabe's grandmother was sitting at the table watching as he prepared the food. Sayetta sat next to her and asked her telepathically about what she was feeling. "I have this peculiar empty feeling in my stomach area. What do you think it could be?"

Smiling gently at Sayetta she said, "It's hunger dear, nothing but good old fashion hunger. The physical body needs to have a certain amount of substance. Then after you eat in about 2-3 hours, your body will need to get rid of what it doesn't need for nourishment. You will need to use the bathroom to do that."

"Ah yes now I remember," she said smiling at Ruth. "It's been a long time between lives. It seems to be coming back to me now. Thank you for your help."

"Not to worry I will be here if you need me."

"Is there anything you don't want me to put in the salad besides meat?" Gabe asked.

"I'm not sure; this body is new to me."

"Okay, I'll put in all of the veggies that I have, and you can just pick out anything that doesn't taste good to you. I think I'll give you olive oil and wine vinegar to use as dressing." He told her.

"I'm sure whatever you fix will be fine."

He placed a bowl of mixed greens on the table along with a small bowl of meat products for himself. Digging the olive oil and vinegar out of the cupboard, he placed them on the table along with some forks and plates.

Sitting down across from her, he bowed his head and gave thanks. "Father says you are welcome for the food." She told him.

He dished up some salad for her and then filled his plate with the greens and helped some meat on top. He picked up the oil and vinegar and drizzled it over both of their salads. He placed the bowl of leftover meat on the floor for Titus. They ate in silence for several minutes.

"I seem to like these vegetables that you have prepared. Titus appears to like his meat too."

They had been communicating mostly telepathically since they had met but he needed to set some ground rules for their partnership. Now was as good a time as any to bring the subject up.

"We need to set some ground rules your behavior here in the physical world. You must start behaving like a regular mortal. Which means you have to speak when you talk to others or when we're in public with other people."

She thought for a moment, "Yes I understand, and that will be better because demons like to get into your head to search for information."

"I need to ask you if you have any powers while in physical form."

"I retain all of my powers; I can change back to pure energy when needed. I can see the future, connect with other angelic beings, use my white light sword and control the minds of a mortal with just a thought. These abilities will remain dormant until I activate them with just a single thought. In my world thought becomes a reality the moment it is formed."

"I'll start arranging the trip tomorrow; I'll need to get things in order before we leave. I'll have my friend come out and stay while I'm gone, she loves to come out to the farm for a little while to think and meditate. She'll love to have Titus for the company and bring her dogs too." He said thinking out loud.

"We need to bring Titus with us. He can detect negatives as well as angels; he will be a big asset for us." She told him.

He seemed surprised hearing the information. " I don't think he's ever been around anything that was negative or angelic besides you."

"All animals can see beyond the physical world to our world. Humans don't give them enough credit. If more people listened to their animals, there would be fewer attachments or attacks by negatives. People are so stupid sometimes, most never think beyond what they can see, feel, hear or touch, when all they have to do is pay attention to how the animal is reacting."

"You'll get no argument from me about that. Okay, we'll take Titus with us. How does that sound to you boy?" He asked the dog not expecting an answer so when he heard the word 'good' pop into his head he nearly fell over. Looking at Sayetta in surprise she nodded her head in confirmation.

"Yes, that was him responding to you. Remember back at the church when I touched you, and you saw the souls?"

"Yes, I remember."

"I was awakening the angelic energy, which resides inside of you. You will start hearing and seeing things you have never seen before in this lifetime."

"That must be why I can see my grandmother now when I have never been able to before. I wonder if it will enhance my writing." He muttered more to himself than her.

"It will help your writing, and you will have new topics to write about."

Finishing dinner Gabe gathered up the plates and put them in the dishwasher.

"I'll give my friend Tish a call and see if she can come out for a couple of weeks. Let me show you the room you'll be using while you're here."

She followed him up the stairs, and down to the end of the hallway where a spacious bedroom was ready for her. She looked at him with a question on her face.

"I always keep this room and the one across from it ready for guests. I sometimes travel for lectures and public appearances, and I don't want Titus to have to travel so much, so Tish comes to dog- house sit as she calls it. You can have this room while you're here it has its own bathroom, television and sitting area." He told her pointing to the different amenities.

"Thank you; I'm sure I'll be comfortable here. Your grandmother says she will help me if I have any questions, so I think I'm all set."

He picked up the remote control for the television and showed her how to operate it. "It's a satellite hookup so you shouldn't have any problems with the reception. If you get bored and want to read, I have a library downstairs which covers a lot of different subjects."

"Thank you; I think I just want to get some rest tonight. Michael or Gabe will be dropping by to see how things are going from time to time so don't mind them; they will just pop in to see me."

"Okay, I'm going to work in my office for a while if you need anything just holler. I think we need to get you some different clothes including a nightgown."

"There's no need for that; I can create my clothes." She told him. Before she finished her sentence, her clothes had changed into a nightgown.

"Wish I could do that, it would make things so much simpler." He said grinning. Leaving her to get settled in he headed for his office.

He sent several emails letting people know he was going to be out of town for a few weeks. He gathered up his laptop, camera, recorder, extra batteries and some notebooks. He called Tish to make sure she was available to come out to the ranch.

Dialing her number, she answered on the third ring.

"Hey Gabe, funny enough I was just thinking about you."

"That makes things easier, are you available for a couple of weeks to come and stay?"

"Of course, you know I love staying there and taking care of the animals. When do you need me?"

"Tomorrow."

"Tomorrow?"

"Yup, let me tell you what happened." He proceeded to tell her everything happened.

"Wow, that's amazing. Will I get to meet her?"

"Yes, but not before we leave, oh, by the way, I'm taking Titus with me this time."

"I'll bet he's in hog heaven if you'll pardon the pun. As you know animals can see spirits, but did you know they are closer to God than we are? They don't have the baggage we have so most of them cross without a problem. You don't see many ghost animals, do you?"

"Now that you mention it, I've never seen one. I've heard stories of animals guarding their charges in England but nothing here. No wonder Titus is following Sayetta around like a puppy. We're leaving early in the morning for Oregon so make yourself at home and bring your fur babies with you. There's plenty of food for you and the dogs."

"I'll be there in the morning sometime, have a good trip and good luck finding the archangel."

"Thanks, see you when we get back. I'll send you and email to keep you updated on our quest." Hanging up the phone, he sat down at the computer and pulled up his writing program. Before he knew it, he was lost in the creation of a new story based on his encounter with Sayetta.

Pulling himself away from the computer, he realized that it was 10 o'clock and he had been writing for three hours straight. No wonder he was stiff when he got up from the chair. Stretching, he went in search of Titus. He found him sleeping outside of Sayetta's bedroom door. "Come on boy, let's go outside." He whispered to the sleeping dog.

Perking up his ears the dog followed Gabe outside. The night was warm and calm; there was a sense of peace on the farm. He made his way to the chicken coop and put extra grain in the feeder, next he went to the corral where his horses were waiting for him. Grabbing a few treats out of the box he spoke softly as he fed them treats. He had the feeling that someone was standing behind him. Turning slowly, he encountered two angelic beings. One he knew was Michael, but he didn't know who the other one was.

"I'm Gabriel; I will be watching over your quest from a distance. I cannot come too close, or I might cause problems with Sayetta."

"I have assigned Gabriel to watch over you both, Sayetta would never allow it, but if she doesn't know, then she can't forbid me to do this," Michael told him.

"I promise I won't say anything or think anything about this. I'm glad to have the extra set of eyes, so to speak."

"You might appreciate the fact that I have chosen your mentor," Michael said.

"What do you mean mentor?"

"In our world, you are a young angel, not yet an archangel, and Gabriel has been mentoring you for several hundred of your years. He chose your name in this lifetime." He said grinning at Gabriel.

"Hey, there's nothing wrong with giving him a strong name is there?" He said grinning back at him.

"Nothing what so ever." Michael agreed.

"Suddenly, I see things I've never seen before. It must be from Sayetta opening me up, isn't it?" he said looking at Gabriel for confirmation.

"Yes, all she did was open your inner eye to the frequency that our world resonates on."

"So, let me get this straight, every plane of existence resonates on a different frequency. That must mean that the physical world, ghosts, angels and demons all have their own frequency." He said more to himself than to them.

"Yes, that's right. We resonate at the highest frequency and demons at the lowest frequency. Those you call ghosts resonate below the angelic realm and the physical world below them. So, you see its quite simple. Negatives cannot enter our realm, but they can enter the others if they manage to find the right frequency. It doesn't happen all that often." Michael told him.

"So, what keeps them from getting into the angelic realm?"

"Our frequency is so high that no matter how much they try they just don't have the ability to resonate that high. For them to get into your world or the realm of ghosts they must either create a dark portal or find a portal where the opening has a lower vibration. Thank goodness those are far and few between." Gabriel explained to him.

"Your gifts will grow and change over the course of the next few weeks," Michael told him.

"It's going to be difficult to summon me without Sayetta finding out," Gabriel told him. He reached out and touched the crucifix Gabe wore around his neck. As he touched the crucifix, Gabe could feel it grow warm against his skin. "Whenever you need me just touch the crucifix and if you have a question, just hold it, and you will be able to hear and speak to me telepathically without Sayetta knowing."

"Great, it nice to know you have my back. So how will I be able to detect the negatives?"

"Before this how did you feel when you were around anything negative?" Gabriel asked him.

"Well whenever I entered a location the air would have a heavy feel to it, and I would feel sick to my stomach. I always get the feeling something, or someone didn't want me there."

"Those are all some of the ways your guardians help you to know there is something negative near you. Now when you encounter something negative, you will know what and where it is. Demons speak in the old language of Aramaic. Your abilities have been heightened so you will understand what they are saying. If you didn't have an angelic soul, and you were a medium you might be able to hear them but not understand what they were saying. Not that it's any great loss, they only ever try to frighten the living anyway. They have such a colorful vocabulary, some of the words they use are ancient, but their meaning is clear." Michael said grinning at him.

"I can well imagine," Gabe said.

"We need to go now and let you get some sleep. From now on you will need to be vigilant, the dark ones know that something angelical has entered your world. They just don't know who or what, but they will be searching for her."

"What happens if they find her, us?" he saw a look pass between the two archangels and was not sure how to interpret it.

"Things could get crazy for a few minutes. You don't want to be physically anywhere near Sayetta when it happens." Michael told him.

"But why? Isn't there anything I could do to help her?"

Gabriel grinned at him and said, "Your best bet is to put some distance between you and them when she finds them, or they find her. It's important she not be distracted by anyone or anything when she has to deal with these beings."

"Okay, I'll remember to get out of the line of fire. What about the angel that resides in me, couldn't he help?"

"If you encounter a demon now that you have contacted your angelic soul it can go one of two ways. Either Zebulon will come forward at the right time and help, or he will come out when he's most vulnerable, and it will end badly. But, don't worry about that, we have both of your backs, and we're never very far away." Gabriel said disappearing.

"Just remember fear and doubt make you vulnerable when dealing with the dark ones. Faith, belief, and prayer are the keys to defeating them. Remember you are never alone, we are always here for you. We have been fighting the dark ones since before the beginning of your world." Michael reassured him and disappeared.

Calling Titus to him, he headed back to the house. Locking the doors and turning out the lights he headed for his bedroom. Changing into sleep pants, he headed for the bathroom to brush his teeth. Finishing his nightly routine, he climbed into bed. Titus jumped up onto the far side of the king size bed making himself at home.

"Good night boy."

Gabe woke to the sound of the alarm going off at 5:30 AM. Throwing on his robe, he headed out to the kitchen to start the coffee. Titus followed closely behind him and headed straight for the kitchen door.

Bumping his nose against the door, he whined to be let outside.

Gabe let him outside and headed for the coffee maker filling the well he added an extra scoop of coffee. He knew he would need several cups before he was awake enough to get everything packed. Just as the coffee finished brewing, he heard Titus scratching at the door to be let in. He could hear movement coming from down the hall, and in the next moment, Sayetta appeared at the entrance to the kitchen. She looked disgustingly well rested which was exactly the opposite of how he felt.

"Good morning Gabe, I had forgotten what it felt like to sleep, restful but peculiar. I don't think I like it much, but I know the physical body requires it."

"I guess I haven't given it much thought; I'm so used to it. I think it would feel strange to you. I guess if I were in your shoes it might make me feel vulnerable."

"Yes, that's the word I was trying to think of. As I could feel my body going to sleep, I grew concerned, and I called out to Gabriel. He informed me that the dark ones know something angelic has entered your world. They just don't know what or where and I'd like to keep it that way for as long as possible." She said with a look of determination on her face.

"I agree, let's keep them in the dark for as long as possible." Getting two mugs out of the cupboard he filled them with coffee and handed her one.

She took a drink and made a face at the taste of it. "It tastes bitter, not at all pleasing." She complained.

"Here, let's try some sugar in it." He said taking the cup from her, he put a teaspoon of sugar in and stirred it handing the cup back to her. "Now try it."

She raised the cup to her lips and took a tentative sip. She smiled at him, "Yes this is much better, thank you." she walked over to the kitchen table and sat down to finish her coffee.

Taking a loaf of bread and a couple of jars of jam out of the refrigerator he made them some toast for breakfast.

Getting the dog food out of the cupboard, he poured some of it into the dog dish. Titus immediately started eating.

Once the toast was done, he put it on a plate and sat it on the table. He grabbed the coffee pot and filled their cups then sat down at the table with Sayetta. They ate in silence for several minutes.

"There are some supplies that we need to pick up before we leave," Gabe told her. "I'll need to stop at Tish's shop and pick up some more white sage and sweetgrass for the trip. I also need to stop at the Walmart Superstore to pick up some batteries, dog food, bottled water and some clothes for you."

"How long do you think it will take us to get to Oregon?"

"At least a couple of days if we take our time. As I'm the only one who will be driving, I don't want to take any chances of becoming overly tired and have an accident. You may be angelic but I'm not, and neither is Titus. Besides we're going to have to get gas, eat and stretch our legs."

"That sounds reasonable. What all are you taking for the trip?"

"I made a list last night." He said pulling a folded piece of paper out of his pocket. "I'll need a still camera, night vision camera, digital recorder, laptop, cell phone, chargers, a couple of blankets, Titus's bed and food, holy water, anointing oil, black salt, crucifix and dried white sage. We can pick up the rest at the store."

"It sounds like you have it all covered. Is Tish your girlfriend, I believe that's the correct term." She asked.

"No, we're great friends nothing more. I would trust her with my life."

"It's always good to have someone you can trust to be there for you. With me, it's Gabriel, Michael, Raphael, Auriel and Ezekiel. We take care of each other."

Finishing his coffee, he washed their dish's and put them back in the cupboard.

"I'm going to feed the animals before I start packing, do you want to come?"

"Yes, I think I would like that."

Heading for the kitchen door, he grabbed a couple of lightweight jackets on the way out. He handed her one of the jackets. "It's a little nippy here in the morning, even though its summer. You'll need the coat."

"Thank you." she said putting the coat on.

He grabbed a small basket from the porch, and they headed for the chicken coop first, collecting eggs and filling the feeder. Next, they headed to the horse barn. Pulling several bales of alfalfa and hay down from the stack he placed them next to the stalls so Tish would have easy access to feed the animals. He placed grain in each of the stall feeders and a couple of flakes of alfalfa. Opening each of the outside stall doors the horses came inside and started eating. Moving to the other side of the barn, he scooped some grain and a couple of flakes of hay in each of the four stalls on the other side opening the outside doors as he went.

"All the animals like it here and they love you." She told him.

"Lord, I hope so, most of the animals here are rescues, and they've been through some rough times, it's about time someone made their lives better." He told her. "Okay everyone's taken care of for now, and Tish will be here later this afternoon and give them their evening feed."

They headed back to the house and Gabe went into his office to grab his equipment and computer. He placed them beside the door leading to the garage. Next, he packed some clothes, grabbed Titus's food, water, bowls and put them with the other things. Going to the basement, he dug out the ice chest and several bottles of water. Setting it in front of the refrigerator, he pulled the well for the ice maker out and dumped the ice into the chest.

Getting his backpack from the closet, he filled it with snacks of every kind. He grabbed a roll of paper towels. Making a quick decision, he opened the ice chest and put the last of his fresh fruit into it. Satisfied that he had everything they needed he opened the inside garage door and carried the ice chest into the garage. He loaded everything into the back of the SUV. He turned to go inside to get the rest of the items and was startled to see Sayetta carrying the rest of the supplies out to him.

"What are you doing, that stuff is too heavy for you!" he fairly shouted at her. "It has to weigh over a hundred and fifty pounds!"

"You must understand, part of my abilities is what you would call superhuman strength." She told him smiling. Setting the items on the garage floor she turned and headed back into the house.

He got the impression that she was treating him like he was a backward child. Taking a deep breath, he released it along with his frustration. It suddenly occurred to him that to the archangels, humans were children. He picked up the items one by one and put them in the car. Checking to see that he had everything he heard a voice coming from behind him. "Don't forget my bed, dad." Titus stood in the open doorway holding his bed and blanket in his muzzle. The voice could only be his, and he realized once again he heard the dog's thoughts.

"*Okay, bring them here, and we can put them in the back seat,*" he replied telepathically. Shaking his head, he wondered if he would ever get used to the idea of being able to communicate with other beings including animals.

Titus came to where he was standing and sat down, patiently waiting for Gabe to take the items from him. Gabe reached out and gently removed the blanket and bed from him and placed them on the back seat. "*It's a good thing I washed your bed a couple of days ago.*" Titus just looked at him with an expression like he didn't understand why Gabe would have to wash his bedding, it smelled alright to him.

Shaking his head at the irony of it all, he headed back into the house to make sure he got everything, lock up the house and put the spare key in the lock box by the front door. "Alright, I think we're all set to go, everybody in the car."

The Journey Begins

Once everyone was in, he activated the garage door opener and backed out. Once out he closed the door and pushed a button on his smartphone to activate the property alarm. Now no one could enter the property surrounding the home and out buildings without setting off the alarm unless you had the code. Tish was one of two people with the code.

Nearing the driveway gate, he pushed the button to open them. The gates slowly swung open. He watched in his rearview mirror to make certain the gates closed. He pulled out onto the main road turning left he headed straight for Tish's small shop. Her shop was located in the heart of Sedona. Arriving at the shop, he parked in front, got out and went inside.

"Gabe, what can I get for you?" she greeted him.

"I need some white sage and some sweetgrass."

Packaging up his supplies she followed him to the door.

"Is that her?" she asked him seeing Sayetta sitting in the SUV.

"Yup, when we get back I'll introduce you. I would now but time is something we're short on right now." He told her.

"Sure, no worries, I'll see you when you get back."

They had been traveling in a comfortable silence for several hours; he could hear Titus snoring in the back seat. "So, do we know where in Oregon this first Archangel is located?" she was quiet for some time, but he had learned to wait for her answer.

"Clackamas, she lives near the Clackamas River. Do you know where that is?"

"I'm not sure; we can look it up on my laptop when we stop to get some lunch."

"Your grandmother says we should stop at exit 106 to get lunch. She says they have good food there and a place for Titus."

"Okay, it's a couple of miles off, but it won't take long to get there."

He finally spotted the exit and noticed an old-fashioned diner sitting at the end of the off ramp. There was a large grassy field behind the diner that would be perfect for Titus. Entering the parking lot, he parked in the area nearest the field. Turning off the engine, he got out and opened the door to let Titus out. Sayetta climbed out of the car, stretched and watched as Titus ran around the field a couple of times. Finally, he settled down enough to go to the bathroom.

"He's a remarkably intelligent and loving dog. I'm of the opinion that if you have an animal in your life, then you are truly blessed. The avenging angel in me hates to see animals abused. If it were up to me, I would personally punish anyone who mistreated an animal. But I must answer to the creator, and it is his will I must do. But there are times when I take great relish in punishing the abusers. I'm supposed to remain neutral but I simply cannot." She told him sighing heavily.

"I hear you; it makes me so mad that I could do to them what they do to the animal. So, I support as many rescue operations as I can. All my animals are rescues, and they always will be." He told her vehemently. He whistled and Titus came running towards him. Opening the back door, he jumped inside and settled on the seat panting heavily. Refilling his water and food bowl, he closed the door leaving the windows down for more air. "We'll be right back big man."

Taking Sayetta's arm, they entered the diner and found an empty booth. Sitting down, he picked up the menu sitting on the table. "Looks like they have a few meat free options. What are you hungry for?" he asked her.

When she didn't answer, he looked up and found her giving him a meaningful look. "Sorry, I forgot you're new to this, so I'll just order for you." He ordered her a cheese omelet, toast, and coffee. "I'll be right back I need to get my laptop out of the car." Returning a couple of minutes later, he opened his laptop and got online. "I'm going to search for the Clackamas River and plan a route."

Pulling up a map of the area, he noticed that the area surrounding the river included Clackamas, Estacada and Oregon City. "Well, it looks like the Clackamas River area covers quite a large area. So how are we going to find her?"

"You need not worry about that, the closer we get to the area the more information I'll receive. Besides I can feel the presence of an Archangel the closer, I get to them." She told him.

He mapped out the route to the area they were headed for and sent it to his smartphone. Checking his phone to make certain the map was there he shut down his computer just as their lunch arrived.

Finishing their lunch Gabe boxed up the leftovers as a treat for Titus at their next rest stop. "I need to pick up some gas then we'll get back on the road." He told her.

Climbing into the car, they headed for the gas station across the street to fill up the car. While the gas was pumping, Gabe got out and washed the windows. Paying for the gas, he climbed back in the car and pulled back out onto the highway.

They traveled for several hours only stopping periodically to get gas and let Titus out. They had traveled several hundred miles, and it was almost sunset.

"I think it's time we found somewhere to stay for the night. I'm going to pull over for a minute and see if I can find a place that takes dogs. I know some Best Westerns take them, I just need to find out if there is one close by." He told Sayetta.

Pulling over to the side of the road, he used his navigation screen to search for the hotel. Fortunately for him, there was one six miles down the road that had openings. Pulling back out onto the highway, he watched for his exit and pulled off the road.

Pulling up in front of the hotel Gabe got out and told Sayetta, "Just wait here, and I'll get us a room."

Heading inside Gabe registered and paid for the rooms. Climbing back in the car, he put it in gear and found a parking spot near their rooms. "I'll get a cart to bring our things in, can you put Titus's leash on him and take him for a walk over there?" he asked her pointing to a small greenway area located at the side of the hotel.

"Of course, but we don't need the leash, he won't leave me."

"I know that, but there is a law here that a leash is required. So, you'll need to put it on him, sorry boy," he said looking at him.

Putting the leash on him, Sayetta walked with him to the greenway.

Gabe found an empty cart and loaded their things on taking it to the room. Coming back out of the room he stopped and watched Sayetta speaking with an older woman with what looked like an older golden retriever. Titus sat down next to her while she was talking with the woman. He watched her bend over and ran her hand over the back of the dog. As she did this, the dog seemed to perk up and licked her hand. He wondered what that was all about. As he watched, Sayetta reached out and took the woman's hand.

Sayetta noticed an older lady walking an old dog who appeared to be having problems walking. "Your spine hurts, doesn't it?" She asked her telepathically.

"Yes, it hurts so much all the time now, can you help me?" the dog asked.

"Of course, bring your owner over here."

The dog changed direction and headed directly for her. The woman holding the leash was surprised at the dog's determination to head for the young woman walking her dog. It was then that she noticed the dog was a large Pitbull and she was fearful it would attack her old dog.

"You needn't worry Titus is a very friendly dog her won't hurt her or you," Sayetta told her.

"How did you know I was worried about that?" the woman asked.

"It was clearly written on your face." She told her smiling.

"Oh, sorry but one does hear stories about that breed of dog." She said apologetically.

"I understand, but you need to realize that it is not the dog but how the dog is treated by humanity that causes the problems. It's like saying all people from Mexico are bad or all Native American's are drunks." She told her sweetly.

"This is Sadie, she's fourteen and doesn't move very well anymore, but she loves traveling, and I always try to take her with me whenever I travel. She just looks at me with those sad eyes if I leave her at home and I can't stand the thought of her being sad."

"I understand, tell me do you believe in angels?"

"My mother always maintained that they walk among us. She always said we need to help others because you never know when you'll encounter an angel. I've lived my life with that idea in mind, although I don't think she ever met one." She said smiling sadly.

"Don't look so sad, your mother Lorraine did indeed meet one in her lifetime."

"How do you know my mother's name?" she asked startled.

"Because I was the angel she met when she was a young woman." As she spoke, her whole being started to glow.

"You're an angel, oh my gosh it's true; you do walk among us. My mother was right!"

"Yes, I have much work to do, but Sadie has asked for healing, and I have agreed to do it." Running her hand from the top of the dog's head to the tip of her tail, she infused healing energy into her. "It is done, she will no longer experience the pain from arthritis that has racked her body. Her spine is healed, and she will be able to get around much better from now on."

Taking Sayetta's hand, she said, "Thank you, thank you God for sending your angel to me." As she touched her hand, she felt a warmth fill her body and a sense of peacefulness fill her.

"The healing is my gift to you for all that you do in the name of the creator."

"You healed me, didn't you? I can feel the warmth filling me."

"Yes, your cancer is healed, you have much work to do. I am charging you with helping spread the word about helping animals. You must also spread the word that Pitbull's are not vicious."

"I will I promise, thank you, what is your name?"

"My name is Sayetta I am an Archangel. I have been given an assignment that is why I am here."

"Thank you, good luck on your mission. Come long Sadie let's go to the room."

The woman and her dog headed back to the hotel and disappeared into one of the lower rooms. As she watched, she noticed that the dog was moving more easily.

"You know you shouldn't do that, it will make it easier for the dark ones to track you." she heard Michael say from behind her.

"Would you have me leave them both to suffer? I think not after all her work for the innocent animal souls." She told him in a haughty manner.

"Now don't get your back, up you know I'm only concerned about your and Gabe's wellbeing. It's more than just you at stake here. You could have called me, and I would have done the healing."

"Do you think that I will let *them* dictate what I do for the creator here in the physical world? I understand the risk I am taking, but sometimes we need to take a risk for the betterment of the soul." She told him sounding very righteous.

He held up his hands as if to ward her off. "You're getting to sound more like Azuriel with every passing century." He told her grinning.

Letting out a big sigh, she smiled lopsidedly, "I guess you're right, I do, don't I? I'm sure he'll be glad to know that all of his teachings did not fall on deaf ears."

He reached out and took her hand, "Let's take a walk I have some news for you."

A Message from Azuriel

As he continued to watch the interplay between the woman, dog and Sayetta he noticed when she touched the woman's hand she was bathed in a luminous glow. The glow seemed to flow into the woman and remained even after she released her hand. They spoke for a little longer than the woman, and her dog returned to the hotel. He was about to leave when Michael suddenly appeared beside her. He sure wished he knew what was going on. He felt someone behind him and turned to find Gabriel standing behind him; it startled him so badly that he almost tipped over.

"Hey what are you trying to do, give me a heart attack?" He said, but Gabriel just smiled at him trying to look innocent. Catching his breath, he asked, "What's up? Can't you give a guy some warning or something?"

"Sorry, I just didn't think about it. I'll try to do better next time."

"So, what just happened with Sayetta and the woman?" He asked his curiosity getting the better of him.

"She did a healing on the woman and her dog." He said frowning.

"Why are you upset, I thought angels did that sort of thing all the time?"

"We do but the fact is every time she uses her abilities it sends a ripple through the world, and the negatives feel it and react by trying to find the source. It's bad enough that the dark ones know something angelic has entered the world without the added stress of her doing a healing to draw attention to herself.

Once they figure out where and what she is, they will stop at nothing to keep her from achieving her goal."

"They can't hurt her, can they? I mean she does have a physical body right now."

"No, the physical body you see is just an illusion, a cloak if you will, to disguise her angelic energy. Just as your body is a temporary home for your soul."

"I guess I never really thought of it that way. But if they can't hurt her, how can they stop her from locating the other archangels and removing the demons?"

"Just because they can't physically hurt her doesn't mean that they can't make things happen in the physical world to slow her down or set obstacles in her way. Remember she has to take physical form to travel and interact in your world, which means those who are assisting her can be injured or killed."

"Wow, I guess I need to be more careful and aware of my surroundings on this trip. I know you'll be here when I need you, but what about the other archangels that were born into a physical body? Won't they be in danger too from these things?"

"Let me tell you something Gabe, the last thing these negatives want is to kill an Archangel in physical form. If they kill the physical body, then they release the Archangel inside and then look out, it's their worst nightmare." Gabriel said grinning.

To Gabe the look on his face spoke volumes, he would relish the ensuing battle that would occur once the Archangel were released. He could almost feel sorry for the demon stupid enough to release an archangel.

"I must go now she is returning," Gabriel said dissolving into nothing.

Turning back to the rail, he noticed Titus heading towards the hotel, pulling Sayetta along with him. He went back into his room leaving the door open. A couple of minutes later he could hear Titus's collar jingling as he approached. Sayetta followed closely behind the dog entering the room looking no worse for wear.

"I see you and Titus made some friends," Gabe said hoping she would further elaborate on what had happened afterward.

"The poor dog could hardly walk, and the woman has done so much to help animals in need that I couldn't leave them like that." She sighed.

"What was wrong with them?"

"The dog had advanced arthritis, and the spine was near collapse. The woman's body was riddled with pain caused by cancer. I healed them both, but Michael got upset with me."

"Why, don't angels do that sort of thing all the time?"

"It's not the healing; it's the fact that in using my powers helps the negatives to track me. They haven't been able to so far, but Michael doesn't want them to know I'm here until it's too late for them."

"Well it was only a short healing, maybe they weren't paying attention." Gabe tried to reassure her. Closing the room door, he turned to open the connecting door between his room and her's. "This is your room," he said entering the adjoining room. "You have your own bathroom, bed, and television. There are extra blankets and pillows in the closet next to the bathroom."

She wandered around the room taking in the clean linen and immaculate bathroom. "This is fine; I'm sure I'll be comfortable here."

"You can rest for a little while if you'd like, then we can get something to eat. In the meantime, I'll give Titus his dinner."

"Maybe I'll do that; I need to report to Ezekiel. I'll see you in a bit."

"Okay, I have a little work to do on my computer." He told her closing the connecting door between the rooms to give her some privacy.

Sitting on the bed, she closed her eyes and summoned Ezekiel. Once the connection was made she opened her eyes, and he stood before her.

"I am on my way to contact the first of our kind. Can you tell me who it is?" she asked him.

"Yes, the first is Auriel." Ezekiel watched her closely to see how she would react to the news. A look of stunned surprise showed on her face.

"I can't believe it, she was always his favorite, and I never thought she would return to the physical world. He must have sent her on a mission." She said fishing for information.

"If she wants you to know why she is here she will tell you. You need to make your way to a place called Oregon City. There you will find a woman named Sara. She is the one you seek, Gabe will know how to find her." He informed her.

"What do you mean Gabe will know how to find her? I'm sure he hasn't a clue, can you give me a little more information? I mean what you gave me is pretty vague. I'm sure there are several thousand Sara's in the state of Oregon and several hundred more just in that city alone."

"The information I have given you should be enough to help you locate her." He said and started to fade from view. "There is one more thing, she removes demons and calls herself a demon seer." He told her and was gone.

"Wow, now I know why people on this side get upset with some of us. Talk about being cryptic and not being more forthcoming with information. I seem to remember a saying about trying to get blood out of a turnip. I wonder if whoever coined the phrase had to deal with Ezekiel." She said more to herself then him. She received a reply that she wasn't expecting.

"I heard that I never said it would be easy." She heard him say.

Shaking her head, she smiled ruefully to herself and headed to Gabe's room to see if he was ready for dinner. She found him hard at work on his computer with Titus sleeping at his feet. She observed him for a few minutes before announcing her presence. She let him know she was there by knocking on the connecting door.

"Hey were you able to get any more information on the person we're looking for?" He asked looking hopefully at her.

"I spoke to Ezekiel, and now I know why you mortals get so upset with some of us. It was like pulling teeth to get anything out of him. He said that you would know how to find her. Her name was Sara, and she lives in Oregon City. I know it's not much to go on, but it's all I have."

"Did he give you any other information like which archangel it was and why she was here?"

"Yes, I do know that its Auriel. She was my teacher and mentor. He didn't say why she was here but did tell me that she is calling herself a demon seer."

"Demon seer, what's a demon seer?"

"It's an old Celtic name for someone who can see, hear, and speak to demons. I can see it would fit perfectly with what she is doing in this lifetime. He told me that she was removing negatives in this life."

"Okay, so here's what we know about her: first we know she's Auriel, she lives in Oregon City, her name is Sara, and she goes by the title demon seer. Let's go get something to eat, and I can think on how to locate her with the information that we already have."

Getting out the dog bowl, he added some food and a treat for Titus. Pulling on his blazer, he grabbed his cell phone and keys. "We'll be back shortly big man so make sure you finish your dinner, and I'll bring you something back." He said ushering Sayetta out the door.

They found a small café a couple of blocks away from the hotel. Placing their order, they discussed various ways in which they might be able to locate the first angel. Their dinner arrived, and the fell silent as they ate. Suddenly Gabe's cell phone rang.

"Hello, oh Hello Tish, how are you settling in?"

"Everything's fine; I just wanted to let you know that I received a strange call just a few minutes ago. Do you remember my friend Sid?"

"Yeah, sure he's the psychic medium that belongs to your paranormal group, nice guy."

"Well, he was doing his morning meditation when an Archangel appeared to him in the meditation. This has never happened before, lower souls sure but not archangels. Anyway, he said his name was Azuriel, and he wanted him to relay a message that is for you alone."

"Hold on a second Tish I need to ask Sayetta about this." Placing his call on hold, he looked up at her and asked, "Do you know an archangel named Azuriel?"

Her expression became serious, and her eyes turned an intense shade of emerald green. "Yes, what is happening?"

"I'll tell you in a minute let me finish hearing what Tish has to say." Taking the phone off hold, he continued his concentration with her.

"Okay, I'm back, what was the message?"

"He said Azuriel told him that he had to give you the message word for word, no ad-libbing. He even made me write it down. Okay, here it is: 'Take heed Demicides has departed.' What does it mean?"

"When I find out I'll let you know, gotta go." He told her said hanging up. "So, who is Azuriel and what does he mean by the message? How come he didn't give you the message himself?"

"Let's get out of here." She said getting up from the table and heading outside.

Leaving the money on the table for the bill, he followed her outside.

She turned to him and said, "We need to talk but not here, let's go back to the hotel." Climbing into the truck, they headed back to the hotel in silence.

Once inside Gabe's room, she started pacing. Titus sensing her energy curled up on his bed and watched her pace. "You're gonna want to sit down and listen carefully." She told Gabe.

Gabe wasn't sure what was going on, but he didn't like the look on her face. Sitting on the bed, he listened as she explained who Azuriel was and what his cryptic message means.

"Azuriel is an archangel who remains in the darkness. He was given permission by the creator to go into the darkness and help any fallen angel who wishes to repent and return to the light. He has a hand full of followers who are with him watching the entrance to the underworld. He keeps his ears open for information and trouble. He rarely leaves his vigil in the darkness, but when he does, then you had better listen to him. He couldn't come to me because that would draw attention to me and my mission, instead he chose to deliver the message by other means that would be less conspicuous."

"What does the message mean and who or what is Demicides."

"He is one of the first of the dark ones. He is very old, very powerful, very nasty and he has left the darkness and is searching for someone, and I think it might be Auriel."

"You mean to tell me he's searching for Auriel too?"

"Yes, it's even more important that we get to her as fast as we can."

"I meant to ask you before, but isn't it unusual for an archangel to be reborn into the physical world? I've never heard of it happening before."

"It does happen occasionally; it's almost unheard of to have more than one in the world at a single time."

"So how did this dark guy find out that Auriel is here in physical form?"

"Evidently she was given the job to remove demons in this lifetime. The ones she has been deporting back to the darkness must have been relaying the information back to Lucifer. Normally he doesn't get involved because he feels it's their own fault for drawing attention to themselves. So, I wonder why Demicides has gotten himself involved. I'll have to check with Michael and find out what he knows. But either way, it's not good for anyone."

"Well if it's as bad as you say I wonder if Auriel is aware that he is hunting for her?"

"How long do you think it will be before we get to where Auriel lives?"

"We should make it there by tomorrow evening. Have you gotten any more information on where her location?"

"I have found out that it's near the Clackamas River. I was told you would be able to find her using the computer. I need to speak with Michael again to find out if he knows about this latest development."

"While you do that I'll take Titus for a walk and then look on the social media sites to see if I can find anything that way. Then I'm going to get to bed so that we can get an early start in the morning."

"Alright, this body is weary, and I think it needs to sleep also." She said heading for her room.

Grabbing the leash, he took Titus out to the green space for a run and to do his business. Inside her room, Sayetta sat on the bed, cleared her mind and called out to Michael.

"Michael, I have need of you."

"I am here." He replied.

She opened her eyes to see Michael standing before her.

"Do you know that Demicides is in the physical world night now searching for Auriel?"

"I am aware of what is going on and keeping my eye on things."

"When were, you going to tell me about it? I had to find out from Azuriel that the dark one was here looking for her."

"Who do you think told him to let you know? Even I am subject to certain rules which I cannot break. Although most of the time I manage to find ways around them."

"Does Demicides know where she is and that I'm here?"

"He waits and watches. Every time she does a removal, it brings him a little closer to finding her. That is why you must find her as quickly as you can."

"Alright, can you give me any more information on her location?"

"You have all the information I can give you. Gabe will find a link to her don't worry Gabriel will help him."

"Sayetta, come here I think I found her." She heard Gabe call from the other room.

"Be there in a moment." She called back

"As I said Gabriel is helping him," Michael said smiling at her and disappearing.

She opened the connecting door to find Gabe sitting in front of his laptop. He looked up smiling as she came in.

"I think I found her, I went to Facebook and searched for 'demon seer' and she's the only one it pulled up. Her name is Sara Lion, here's a picture of her come and take a look."

Standing behind Gabe, she looked over his shoulder at the monitor just as he was enlarging her picture. The moment she saw the picture she could see Auriel's image superimposed over the picture. "Yes, that's her. Is there a way to contact her?"

"How do you know it's her, you've only seen a picture?"

"You see the physical body image; I see the soul image."

"Oh, okay. We can contact her by private message, but some people don't always look at their Facebook messages every day. It looks like she has a website, maybe there's a contact page there." He said clicking the link displayed on the page and he was brought to the website. Clicking on the contact page, he sent a short email with his phone number.

"There," he said pressing the enter button and sending the email. "That's about all we can do for tonight. Let's get some sleep; we have a long drive again tomorrow."

"Alright, I guess if that's all we can do we'll just have to wait. Everything moves so slowly here in the physical world. I think it would drive me crazy if I had to spend much time here. It suits her you know." She commented heading back to her room.

"What suits her?" he asked.

"Her name, Auriel it means lion of God." She told him closing the door.

He was unaware of the meaning of Auriel's name, but now it all made sense. He had to agree with Sayetta; waiting wasn't his favorite thing to do either. A soft whine broke into his thoughts. He looked over to see Titus sitting next to the bed asking if he could sleep with him. "Okay, but no pushing me out of bed or you'll have to get down." He told him.

The dog proceeded to jump up on the far side of the king size bed and curl up into a ball. He looked at Gabe with big sad eyes, and he grinned. '*That dog really knows how to work those eyes."* He thought to himself grinning. As if on cue Titus twitched his eyes in Gabe's direction, and knew he was sunk. Shaking his head, Gabe gathered his nightclothes, toiletries, and razor heading into the bathroom.

In her room, Sayetta decided she would get some sleep as the physical body she had created was growing weak with fatigue. She decided to try sleeping like a mortal and pulled back the covers and climbing into the bed. The bed was cool yet oddly comforting. Before she knew it, she had dozed off in a revitalizing sleep.

In the next room, Gabe finished getting ready for bed and decided to spend some time updating his blog. He spent the next 45 minutes blogging about his upcoming book and answering some fan mail. Turning off his computer, he crawled into bed and was soon asleep.

Lucifer Interferes

On the angelic plane, Michael and Gabriel were deep in conversation.

"And when were you going to tell me Demicides had left the darkness and entered the physical realm?" Gabriel asked Michael.

"I knew it was only a matter of time before you found out, you always manage to have eyes and ears everywhere. Besides he's still trying to find her. Although, I'm still trying to figure out how he knew Ariel had returned to the physical world. It seems like there may be a leak somewhere."

"Agreed, but it can't be, much of a leak otherwise he would already know where she is. I'm betting that the only reason he knows she's here is because of the demons that she's deported back to hell. Fortunately for us, they don't understand the concept of time and place otherwise he would know exactly where she is." Gabriel reasoned.

"Good point, Sayetta should arrive there tomorrow evening. I'll get a hold of Sara and let her know that someone is coming and she should make sure she meets them."

"I had almost forgotten how close you and Auriel are, even when she's in the physical world," Gabriel said giving Michael a meaningful look. It was widely known in the angelic realm that Auriel and Michael were soulmates and whenever she was in the physical body, he was sure to be close by.

"Sara just went to bed, but she's not asleep, yet so I'll go and speak with her now."

"Alright I've got to go myself, Ezekiel needs my help with a new trainee."

Sara had just gotten into bed and was dozing off when she heard Michael calling her name.

"Sara, Sara wake up, I need to speak with you."

"Can't it wait until morning, I'm tired?" She asked him telepathically.

"No, it can't. You know I would never wake you up if it wasn't important." He reminded her.

"Yes, Michael I know. So, what's up?" she asked sitting up on the side of the king size bed trying not to disturb her three dogs as they slept at the foot of the bed.

"There is a man named Gabe who is trying to get a hold of you. You must call him as soon as you can."

"Okay, what does he want?"

"You will have to wait until you speak with him. I can tell you nothing more."

"Can't or won't?" Hannah, Sara's guardian angel, chimed in.

"That's a valid question, Michael." Sara agreed.

"I *really* hate it when the Arch's go all cryptic on us." Ann, Sara's spirit guide interjected.

"Silence you two!" Michael warned them sharply. "It's not that I won't but rather that I can't at this moment." He informed them.

"Ah, now I understand. Alright, it will have to wait until I talk to this Gabe person then." She said and crawling back into bed and going fast asleep.

"Are you sure you can't give us even a little hint Michael," Hannah asked.

"No, you'll find out soon enough." He told her breaking contact.

"I'll bet this has something to do with Auriel otherwise why wouldn't he tell Sara?" Ann asked.

"I would have to agree, but why would he keep anything from Auriel? Oh well, it must be something she's not going to like." Hannah reasoned.

"Agreed we'll just have to wait for the phone call, how I hate waiting," Ann complained.

The night passed quickly, and Demicides continued his search, waiting and watching for the next time Auriel was active. She was disrupting and removing too many of Lucifer's workers here in the physical world, and his patience was wearing thin. He had to do something to stop her. Granted she had been doing this for quite some time and up until this point, she was only a minor annoyance. But a few moments ago, he had been summoned by Lucifer. He knew that Lucifer never bothered with you unless you had done something to annoy or anger him, either of which did not have a good outcome for the individual.

Kneeling before Lucifer, he could tell he was not in a good mood. Who was he kidding, Lucifer was never in a good mood, but you could see he was visibly trying to keep his anger in check.

"Master, you requested my presence."

"Yes, what took you so long?" He snarled.

"I came as soon as you called master."

"Not fast enough." He shouted, his voice echoing in the darkness. "Why am I getting reports of an increased amount of deportations from the physical world?"

"I don't think there has been too much of an increase, maybe a handful that's all."

"Don't contradict me!" Lucifer lashed out at him. "If it were only the younger more inexperienced souls and minions, then I would say it's their own stupidity that caused their return, but it's not just them." he ground out through clenched teeth.

"I have not been made aware of any old ones that have entered the physical plane lately being deported."

"Then you are failing in your duty to me and that I cannot tolerate."

"But we have no need to enter the physical world master; it is beneath us."

"That is true; we rarely bother ourselves with that particular plane of existence. But I am not talking about that. Do you remember what happens to those who go against my will?"

How could he forget he thought to himself? No one wanted to end up entombed in the planet below to spend eternity in isolation with only the living souls above to try to influence? "Yes, master I know, but what has that to do with me? I would never let them out."

"*Silence!*" Lucifer shouted.

Demicides could feel the whole of the dark world shudder in response to Lucifer's anger. Even those souls who constantly cried out in pain were silent. The silence was something that was rarely heard here in what the humans called hell.

"Auriel has returned to physical form and has just removed one of the offenders from his prison. I will not have them released!" he growled.

"No master of course not."

Lucifer got up from his throne and started pacing; even his guards stood back in fear of what he might do next.

"Did I complain when she removed the minions or the lesser souls? Well maybe a little, but I figured it was their own fault for being stupid enough to get in her way. But she has gone too far. I imprisoned him because he went against my laws. What gives her the right to free him by sending them back here? Now I must deal with him all over again. He seeks my forgiveness, telling me he will never go against me again. I know this is a lie, they never learn, I never did, and they are less than me."

"What would you have me do master?"

Stopping he turned to face him. "You will go to the physical world, find Auriel and stop her from deporting anymore of the offenders that I have imprisoned in the earth."

"But master how am I to achieve this?"

"I don't care how you do it just do it I shouldn't have to do your thinking for you! If you fail me, I won't even bother imprisoning, you. Do you understand me?"

"Yes, master." He knew exactly what that meant. Lucifer would destroy him.

"Well, what are you waiting for? Get out!"

"But master, how will I find her? The physical world is vast, and I don't even know where she is or what she looks like."

"Fool, must I do everything for you? Every time she deports one of the minions or lesser souls you should be able to locate her by the disturbance when she does a removal. Now leave me before I lose what little patience I have left."

"Yes master, I will not fail you." Turning, he left the throne room. '*Crap*' he thought, '*why me, why can't he just leave me alone in my misery. I always suspected he didn't like me and now I know sure.*' How was he going to do this? She was too strong for him. His only chance might be to kill the physical body. But then once the body is dead Auriel will be released and she'll come after him. There was no way that he could win. Better to deal with her then what Lucifer has in mind for him if he fails. Shaking his head as if to clear it he headed towards the nearest dark portal to enter the physical plane.

Little did he know that a lesser soul had been listening to the early part of his conversation with Lucifer. She knew she had heard enough of the conversation to know she had to leave before they caught her. She snuck way while Lucifer was ranting, and headed for where Azuriel kept vigil. She was greeted by the two archangels who guarded Azuriel.

"I seek an audience with Azuriel; I have information."

Azuriel turned and beckoned the soul closer.

"What information do you have for me?" He asked her.

"I need something in exchange for the information I have." She told him.

"Give me the information and I will see what I can do to help you."

"You promise? I know you always keep your promises." She reminded him.

"I always do." He confirmed.

"Demicides has been sent by Lucifer to find Auriel; he said she is in physical form right now."

"Why would he send him to find her?"

"She deported one of the old ones Lucifer had imprisoned in the earth, and he's very upset."

"Do you know what Demicides intends to do?"

"No, I'm sorry I got scared they would find me, and I left before the end of the conversation." She said shaking her head and looking down in shame.

"You were brave to listen for as long as you did, thank you for the information. Are you ready? You know you will have to answer for what you have done?"

"Yes, and I am ready to take whatever punishment I need to for a chance to be in the light."

"Very well," touching her shoulder she was transported to the light where Ezekiel waited for her.

"Welcome home child." He greeted her.

"Thank you; it's good to be home again." She told him smiling as if a weight had been lifted from her.

"You do realize that you will have to answer for the decisions you have made?"

"Yes, I understand that I have to atone for what I have done and the decisions I have made, and I am ready to do it." She told him a look of fear and resolution on her face.

"Child, you have nothing to fear, this is not hell." He told her with a smile.

"Yes, I know." She said smiling nervously at him.

He led her away, and they disappeared.

Angelic Rescue

Gabe awoke at 5:30 am the next morning; his body clock just would not allow him to sleep past that time unless he was sick. Throwing the sheet back, he climbed out of bed and headed for the bathroom. Closing the door, he took a quick shower, looking in the mirror he decided to forgo shaving and grow a beard. It had been a couple of years since he had last worn one.

Opening the bathroom door, he noticed Titus was still sound asleep. He walked over and nudged him, he groaned and blinked open his eyes.

"Time to get up sleepy head, we have a long way to go."

Titus stretched lazily and slowly climbed off the bed. He wandered over to his water dish and got a long drink. Grabbing his jogging clothes out of the suitcase he got dressed put on Titus's leash and headed out the door for a run.

In the room, next door Sayetta heard Gabe leave for his run. She decided she would take a shower although she didn't need one, but she thought the experience would be good for her. Ruth, Gabe's grandma, appeared before her.

"Let me show you how this works." Going in to the bathroom, she pointed to the small bottles of shampoo and conditioner provided by the hotel. "The one marked shampoo is used to clean your hair. This is used to clean your body. Here I'll show you." She sent an image telepathically to her to show her what to do.

"Ah, I understand now, thank you, Ruth."

"You're welcome if you need me call me." she said disappearing.

Sayetta dissolved the clothing she was wearing and turned the shower on adjusting the temperature before she got in, as Ruth had shown her.

The feel of the water cascading over her body felt curiously soothing. Washing her hair and body, she rinsed off and toweled dry. Materializing another set of clothes, she was just in time to hear Gabe come back. In the next moment, she heard his shower and knew it would be a few minutes before he was out. Going outside, she walked several blocks looking at the area and the people. There were people walking, riding bicycles and jogging. Some wished her a good morning while others simply focused on what they were doing.

A rather scruffy looking dog came towards her. Its coat which was once white was brown with dirt, and its body was painfully thin. But it was her eyes that spoke to Sayetta; they were a deep golden yellow. She looked to be the same breed as Titus. She called the dog telepathically to her.

"Where is your home?"

"I don't have a home, I had one but the old man died, and no one wanted me." She said sadly.

"What is your name little one?"

"I used to be called Lucy."

"Do you like the name, if you do then Lucy it shall be."

"I like it because my man named me and he was a gentle soul."

"How would you like to come with me?"

"Do you mean to heaven? I mean you're an angel, aren't you?"

"No little one, you have many years to be here. I have a friend who lives on a ranch, and he has another dog just like you. He is also a gentle soul and will take great care of you."

"I think I would like that, what about the other dog do you think it will be okay with him?" she asked anxiously.

"His name is Titus, and he will gladly welcome you." she told her smiling gently.

"Then yes, I will go with you, can we go to the ranch now?"

"We can go but not to the ranch right now we are on a journey to find another archangel. Once we find her, then we will return to the ranch."

"Okay, I don't care as long as I can go with you." she said happily.

"Let's go to where I am staying, and we can get you cleaned up." She told her turning back the way she had come.

Michael appeared walking beside her, "Another cause?" he asked her.

"No another precious soul saved. Michael this is Lucy." She said introducing her to him. "Lucy this is Michael."

"Hello, Lucy."

"Hello Michael, you're an angel, too aren't you?" She asked.

"Yes, I understand you need a good home, and Sayetta has found you an excellent one. You will love the ranch and all of the other animals." He assured her.

"I wanted to let you know that I spoke to Sara last night and she will be watching for the message from Gabe. I did not tell her anything more than that she needs to call as soon as she gets the message. I will leave it up to you to explain the situation."

"Thanks, one question, does she know who resides within her?"

"Yes, it's been several years since she found out who her soul belongs to. She is one of the few who embraces and understand what it means to have the soul of an archangel. I had to help Auriel to understand that she cannot take over the physical consciousness unless called upon. As you know, that is very hard for her to acquiesce to."

"Yes, I can see where it would be very hard for her. Having trained under her, I know patience is not her strong point." She agreed with a knowing smile.

"On a more sobering note, you are now aware that *he* has entered the earthly plane. But what you do not know is that he and Auriel have a history together. She was forced to return him to the darkness when all she really wanted to do was to eradicate him from existence."

"What really happened between the two of them? There are rumors, but I never put stock in any of them." She told him.

"It happened several hundred years ago, *he* was given a task by Lucifer, and *he* failed to accomplish it. As you know, Lucifer is not the most tolerant of beings. In his anger, he imprisoned Demicides in an earthly tomb."

"Do you know what the task was?"

"I am not at liberty to tell you at this time, but he was imprisoned for a couple of hundred years. When Hitler came to power, Lucifer let him out and sent him to influence Hitler to commit genocide. He won his freedom by succeeding but was cast back down by Auriel for his success. Needless to say, he was furious."

"I understand now, but do we know why Lucifer has sent him in search of Auriel."

"I can't say for certain but there was an incident several months ago, that comes to mind, Sara was called to a house that had demonic activity. She sensed one of the old demons. Auriel put out her feelers and sensed the demon residing in the ground; it tried to push Sara and 2 of the members of her team down a flight of stairs. She brought Auriel forward and drew the demon out of the ground right into Gabriel and my arms. Boy, was it pissed. She made it tell her why it had been imprisoned in the earth. Then we cast it back down; I'm sure Lucifer wasn't happy about that."

"Well, I can see where that would upset him a bit, to say the least. I take it *he* doesn't know where to find her?"

"No, she masks herself well, unfortunately, every time she does a removal it sends a ripple through our plane of existence. It doesn't affect us, but the darkness feels it and moves in the direction of where ripple came from. Fortunately for her, it's hard to locate the focal point of the disturbance. That's the reason *he* hasn't found her yet."

"Well, then we had better make sure that we reach her before *he* does," Sayetta said with a grim look on her face.

"Agreed, you had better let Gabe know what's going on. He needs to be kept in the loop. I'll see you later I have some unfinished business to attend to." Michael said disappearing.

The dog standing beside her nudged her leg for attention. "Alright Lucy, let's get back to the hotel."

Arriving back at the hotel, she had Lucy wait in her room while she went in to talk to Gabe. Knocking on his door, she waited for an answer.

"Come in."

Opening the connecting door, she found him once again in front of his computer. "I have some news for you."

"Well I hope its good news, but I kind of doubt it." He said turning around in his chair to look at her.

"Well actually, I have good news and bad news." She told him smiling ruefully at him.

"Okay give me the good news first."

She walked back to the connecting door and opened it. Sitting in the doorway, Gabe could see a dirty Pitbull.

"Her name is Lucy, and she's come to live with you and Titus. Her owner was an old man that died, and she's been living on the streets as you can see. I'm going to give her a bath and some food."

"Okay, do you think she'll get along with Titus?"

"Of course, Titus come and meet your new sister." She called to Titus.

Titus who had been sleeping on the bed raised his head at the mention of his name and climbed down. He padded over to where Sayetta was standing next to

Lucy. He reached out with his nose and sniffed Lucy's ear, and she sniffed him back.

"You see, they like each other, you need each other."

"Alright, so what's the bad news?" He wanted to know.

She recounted her recent conversation with Michael.

"Well, I had a feeling it wouldn't be as easy as I hoped it would be. So, what happens if *he* finds her before we do?"

"It depends on Sara. I feel if she is already removing demons then her skills are advanced enough to protect her from the average run of the mill demons. The problem is, this is not your average lesser demon; this is one of the old ones. She should be able to sense it coming and put up her white light protective field. The older ones are very clever, not like the lesser demons and minions. If she's not very good at detecting them, then she won't be ready for it, and the result would be disastrous for her in more ways than one." She told him ominously.

"What does Michael say about Sara?"

"He's rather reluctant to say much since he is not supposed to interfere with our mission."

"Well, maybe he needs to be a little more forthcoming with information," Gabe said in frustration. He got up and started pacing the room; the dogs followed him with their eyes as he moved back and forth. "Okay so we know she's advanced, we just don't know how advanced. We know she's already removing demons, so she has some skills." He mused.

"We'll just have to get to her before *he* does." She told him grimly.

"Alright, you bathe Lucy while I get everything together. Once she's bathed, I'll feed her and get everything into the car." Gabe told her.

Ten minutes later Lucy was bathed, and towel dried. Gabe fed both dogs and started loading everything on the baggage cart he had found down the hall.

Having finished their food Sayetta took both dogs down to the green space next to the hotel and let them relieve themselves. By the time, they were through Gabe had everything loaded in the car, checked them out of the hotel and was waiting for them.

Opening the car door, the dogs quickly jumped into the back seat and laid down together. They climbed into the car and entered the freeway. They had been driving for over an hour when Gabe's phone rang. Hitting the answer button on the steering wheel, he answered the phone.

"Gabe here,"

"Hello Gabe this is Sara, what can I do for you?"

"I think that it's the other way around it's something we can do for you."

"It must be something very important for Michael to intervene."

"It is, I am on my way to see you. I have someone with me that you need to speak with, her name is Sayetta."

Speaking in the angelic language, Sayetta introduced herself. "Auriel, come forth, it is I Sayetta, your friend."

On the other end of the phone, Sara felt a shift in her consciousness. It was the same thing that happened to her whenever Auriel came forward to deal with a demonic. She could hear herself answering in the same language. This was the first time something like this had ever happened. She could understand what they were saying just as she could understand what the demons were saying when they were speaking Aramaic. She felt like she was listening in on a private conversation.

"Sayetta old friend, why have you sought me out?" Auriel asked.

"Lucifer has sent Demicides to find you and stop you from removing the demons who are imprisoned. You must have released one he had imprisoned in the earth and sent it back to him."

"Yes, Michael, Gabe and I had the pleasure of sending one back a couple of months ago. My first in this form, but hopefully not the last." She said laughing.

"I need to speak with your physical consciousness so that I may help prepare her for the upcoming conflict. Michael is not very forthcoming with the information I need here in the physical world regarding Sara."

"Ah, I understand, Michael likes to go by the rules, whereas I was always a rule breaker. He can be quite a stickler about it sometimes. So be it, I will retreat and let you speak with her." She retreated into the back of Sara's consciousness, and Sara was once again in charge.

"Sara, do you hear me?"

"Yes, I hear you. Do you have something to write my address and phone number down on?"

"Just a minute," Gabe pointed to the glove compartment where she found a tablet and pencil. "Alright, I'm ready." She wrote the information down.

"Do you know what time you'll be getting here?"

"I'm not sure; we hope to be there before dark."

"Give me a call when you get closer, and I'll guide you to my house. I have a farm in the country, and my home is not easy to find even if you have a GPS."

"Okay, we'll give you a call when we get closer," Gabe told her.

Gabe pushed the button on the steering wheel to end the phone call. "Let's look for a place to have breakfast and let the dogs stretch their legs. Keep your eyes open for dining signs."

It took them another half hour to find a suitable place to stop and eat. Pulling into the parking lot they garnered a spot on the side of the building where there was a small vacant lot that was for sale. Sayetta opened the door and let the dogs loose. They immediately started running around and playing with each other. She let them play for several minutes then told them telepathically that they needed to go to the bathroom before they went back into the car.

They obediently found a place to relieve themselves and came running back to where she stood with the car door open. Gabe rolled down the windows so they could get some fresh air but it was still rather hot out and no trees for shade. Just as the thought occurred to him, Sayetta raised her hand in the air, and a small cloud seemed to come out of nowhere and move into position right above the car blocking it from the intensity of the sun.

She gave him a knowing smile and started towards the restaurant. Shaking his head, he followed her into the building.

"That was a neat trick, care to teach it to me?" he asked her with a grin.

"Sorry, but you would have to die to learn that one." She said smiling in response.

"Well, I guess that must wait, at least for a little while."

The hostess came over, and Gabe asked to be seated next to where their car was parked.

Gabe pulled out his cell phone and entered the information for Sara's home and phone.

"I should have asked her if she had any removals planned in the next couple of days, but I completely forgot," Gabe said.

"That's okay; I'll ask Michael if he knows." Connecting telepathically with Michael she asked, 'Does Sara have any removals planned in the next 24 hours?'

"She does have a removal this afternoon but its nothing to worry about." He responded.

The waitress came to take their order and bring them something to drink.

"He says she has a removal this afternoon, but it's nothing to worry about."

"What does he mean there's nothing to worry about?"

"It means that the demonic she is going after is either a minion or a lesser demon, obviously, something she can handle."

"Isn't there a risk involved in any removal? Why can't the archangels just go into the darkness and take control of the demoniacs'?"

"Well its their home turf as you say, and no one knows it better than them. No archangel would venture into their plane by themselves; there is a risk of attack or worse. We cannot risk them following us and finding out where our doorways are. They are unable to sense the portals that lead to our world like they can with the physical world portals."

"It's sort of a catch 22, darn if you do and darn if you don't. But what about Azuriel, he stays there all the time you said?"

"Azuriel is not alone; there were twelve other archangels who went with him to help and watch over him. They would not dare to go against him, the repercussions from the attack would send the avenging archangels into the darkness, and those who attacked him would be eradicated. It would cause open warfare again, and I don't think anyone wants that, not even Lucifer."

Their breakfast arrived, and they spent the next 30 minutes eating. Gabe set aside some meat as a treat for the dogs. Once finished, they headed back to the car. Opening the back-door, Gabe gave each dog their treats.

Climbing in the car, they pulled back onto the freeway. "I estimate we should be in Clackamas in three and a half hours," Gabe said.

"Is that a long time? I'm still having problems trying to understand the concept of time."

"Not really, it's a relatively short period."

Sara's Arrival

They had only gone a few miles when Michael connected with Sayetta telepathically.

"Sayetta, Sara just informed me her removal is in Lebanon today. Gabe needs to call her and let her know that you'll be meeting up with her in Lebanon. I think you both need to go with her on this removal so you can see where her abilities are. She's already on her way there."

"Gabe, Michael just told me that Sara's removal is in Lebanon. How far is that from where we are now?"

"I'm not sure; I'll have to look it up." Pushing a button on the steering wheel, he said, "Maps, show me Lebanon, Oregon." The map appeared on the small screen. "GPS, route to Lebanon, Oregon.

"Forty-five minutes to destination." The GPS announced.

He pushed the call button "Call Sara" re-requested. It responded, "Calling Sara" the phone rang a couple of times, and Sara answered.

"What's up Gabe, I didn't expect to be hearing from you so soon; I'm on the road right now."

"I know, Michael told us you are headed for Lebanon, we'll meet you there. When we get in town, we'll find a restaurant and let you know where it is."

"Okay, must be something important if Michael in wanting us to meet first, alright I'll be waiting for your call." She hung up.

Gabe breathed a sigh of relief. "Well, at least she wasn't upset by us changing her plans."

"She's probably used to the changes in plans when you work with us plans can change at a moment's notice. You always did complain about it in your other lives, but you got used to it then and you will again." She told him a matter of factly.

They arrived in Lebanon less than an hour later and found a small café not far off the freeway. Parking in the lot they took the dogs across the street where a small park was located. Letting them run for several minutes they gave them some food and water. Once they had the dogs settled, they made their way into the café. After being seated Gabe text, Sara, the name and location of the café.

Looking over the menu, they ordered, and Gabe heard his phone notification go off. Picking up his phone, he saw the response from Sara letting him know she got the message.

"So, what exactly are we going to be doing with Sara?"

"I will be observing her and gauging where she is with her abilities as well what she needs help with."

"You mean you can tell that just by watching her work?"

"Yes, and when Auriel comes forward, I can see how she works through Sara. You'll need to keep your senses open."

"This should be very interesting to witness. Do you think she'll let me film it?"

She laughed, "You're still thinking like a human, but yes I think she'll let you film it."

They spent the next hour talking and getting to know each other better. Suddenly Gabe's phone went off, and he saw it was a text from Sara letting him know she was just pulling off the freeway. A couple of minutes later a black Kia Soul pulled up in front of the café and a woman of around thirty got out of the car. She was around average height with a figure that was fuller than was conventional but suited her. Gabe stood up and went to greet her.

"You must be Gabe," Sara said holding out her hand.

Gabe took her hand, and the moment he touched her hand, he felt an electrical-like current pass between them. From the look on her face, he knew that she was experiencing the same thing he just felt.

"Sayetta is waiting at the table." He told her leading her to their table.

Arriving at the table, Sayetta stood up and held out her hands to Sara. Taking her hands, they hugged. Sayetta had her back to Gabe, but he could see Sara's face clearly. He was amazed at what he saw; her face was transformed. Eyes the color of white shown out of a face so stunningly beautiful that it hurt to look at her. The transfiguration only lasted a few seconds, and then Sara's face was there again.

"Come let us sit," Sayetta said motioning to the booth they were seated.

"It's so good to see you again sister, it seems like an eternity since I have seen you," Sara said, using the ancient Aramaic, but the voice was still Auriel's.

"Too long sister, I have been given a task to do for Him. And it must be done with all speed."

"I see you have Zebulon with you as usual," Auriel said. "How is he adjusting to the physical world in this lifetime?"

"Easier than in his last lifetime. He seems more open to us, so maybe he's getting used to the change."

Auriel burst out laughing, "It is something that you never really get used to. I've been lucky all my physical lives have adapted to me. Although the individual lives have not been all sunshine and roses." She told her ruefully. "But enough about that, why have you come to me?"

Auriel explained the reason behind her arrival in the physical world. After she had finished, Auriel was quiet for a few moments. "Well, it sounds like you could use some help finding the other seven of us. But I have a feeling you haven't told me everything."

"Yes, that's true, but we will talk about it later, right now I need to talk to Sara."

"Very well, we can speak later." Auriel agreed retreating into Sara's subconsciousness.

"Well that was interesting, she usually doesn't come forward like that, not even when Michael is here. Unless of course, we are in the presence of negatives." Sara told Gabe and Sayetta. "It's taken me a long time and a lot of frustration to get her under control. Michael has helped me a lot. Her consciousness was coming forward at inappropriate times. Her attitude towards humanity was another issue that has been plaguing me for years. She finally realizes that I must live in the physical world, so she needs to be less autocratic and nasty to people. People don't realize what sleeps inside of me. If they're nasty to me, she feels they are nasty to her and that she will not tolerate."

"You heard what I told Auriel?" Sayetta asked.

"Yes, when my consciousness shifts to the back I can still see and hear everything that goes on. I would welcome any help you can give me improving my abilities. Michael has told me that I've barely scratched the surface of my abilities."

"I agree with Michael you have more to learn and I will gladly help you. I will also be helping Gabe to release his abilities."

"Would you like to get something to eat or drink?" Gabe asked her.

"I would kill for a cup of coffee."

"Coffee it is then," Gabe said motioning for the waitress. "Could we get another coffee and cream please."

"Sure, I'll be right back." The young waitress said and promptly returned with creamer and a cup of coffee.

Adding cream and sugar, Sara took a deep drink of the coffee and let out a blissful sigh. "Oh, that's good, I needed that." She said taking another long drink of coffee. "So about today? Are you going along to observe how I do my removals?"

"Yes, Gabe and I will observe the removal process. I will cloak the both of us so that we can observe and not interfere with your removal process."

"Alright, I know there is more to your visit than you have told either Auriel or myself, but I understand there is always a reason for that." Sara told her.

"You both are right, but this is neither the time or the place for the rest of the information. When we arrive at your place, I will explain everything in detail. So, what have you been called in to do today?" Sayetta asked.

"I received a message last night about a man being constantly attacked by a negative entity in his home. Evidently, this has been going on for some time. He says that there are actually two entities in his home and negative one and another that has been visiting him off and on while his mother was alive. He says that this one looks like a giant lizard man and it's wearing a red cloak. I don't get the feeling that the lizard-man is negative. Lebanon has a strong Native American history, and in some of the local cultures the lizard-man would be a protector rather than a negative."

"This should be interesting, I've heard about these creatures who watch over people who are of Native American descent. Is your client of Native American heritage?" Gabe asked curiously.

"I'm not sure, that's a good point, I guess I'll have to ask him when I get there. Let me finish my coffee, and we'll head over to his place."

"Sara, we will be watching but not taking part. I am not to interfere only observe unless it is life threatening." Sayetta informed her.

"Oh, alright, you're just an observer at this point then?"

"Just for this particular encounter. We are here to observe how the removal process affects you physically, emotionally and mentally."

"Ah I see, thank you for doing this. I believe I'm handling it well, but I may be too close to the situation to see if it's taking a toll on me. Sometimes it takes someone from the outside to get a fresh perspective on things. I have a friend who came to me one day with some concerns. He told me there were people in the local paranormal community that were making comments about me. He told me that he believed Auriel was coming out more than I was aware of. He also noticed a distant and superior attitude that was never there before. I enlisted the help of Michael to make Auriel realize how her attitude was reflecting on me here in the physical world and causing me to acquire a negative reputation. She understood, and it has not been a problem since then. Although once in a while she gets her back up if someone treats me bad."

"I can understand her being upset if you're not treated with respect, I don't like it either." Sayetta told her.

Sara finished her coffee and asked, "So, how are we going to do this?"

"We'll follow you to the client's house and park at the end of the block. Then I'll cloak us, so the neither the living or the dead will know we're there. Once we are cloaked, we will be able to observe everything that happens. When you're through with the removal, we can meet back at the café." Sayetta told her.

"Alright let's get going then, I told them I would be there by two, and it's 1:45 now." She said gathering up her purse.

Gabe stopped to pay the bill and followed Sara out of the café. "Which car is yours?" he asked.

"The black soul," she said pointing to the car on the far side of the entrance. There was a website decal on the back of the hatch which read www.demonseer.com in bold white lettering. "It's ironic, but I didn't even think about the name; I just liked the car because it had enough room for my dogs."

Gabe and Sayetta laughed at the thought of the black soul and thought how appropriate it was for her. "I need to let the dogs out for a few minutes then we can go," Gabe said.

Letting the dogs out of the car, they immediately ran over to Sara and licked her hands. "They know a soft touch when they see one." she laughed reaching down to fondle their ears. "Go and potty you two so we can go." She told them. They seemed to understand and headed for the grassy area.

Five minutes later they were headed for the client's house. Once they saw Sara's car pull into the driveway of the house, they drove past it and parked at the end of the block.

"Gabe don't get out yet; I'll let you know when it's safe."

Turning to the dogs, she told them, "You need to be very quiet, no barking or whining no matter what you see until we return. Nothing can harm you while you are under my protection."

They agreed to be silent until she returned. Placing her hands on the dashboard, Sayetta let out a burst of energy that almost blinded Gabe.

"It's done, we can leave the car now, no one will see us or the vehicle." Climbing out of the car, they started back towards the house where Sara was parked. She was sitting in the backyard at a small table speaking with a man and a woman. They moved closer to hear what was being said.

She held out her hand to the man and woman she introduced herself. "Hello, I'm Sara."

"Please sit down, my names Tyler and this is my girlfriend, Trina," Tyler said gesturing to the table and chairs set up in the small grassy area by the driveway.

"So, tell me what's been happening." She asked them.

"My mother and I moved here eleven years ago. At first, everything was quiet; then we began seeing shadows out of the corners of our eyes. We would hear voices, but no one was around. There was chanting at night in the garden area down by the creek. Then my mother woke me up screaming one night. She said she saw this lizard person it was wearing a red cloak. It was standing over her in the night when she woke up; it went on for several years. After she had died, I didn't see it for a while. Then I started feeling something dark and evil around me. Shortly after I began feeling this negative entity around me, I started hearing chanting; I think it's the Indians." Tyler told her.

"What makes you think there are Indian spirits here?" Sara asked.

"This whole area belonged to the Northwest tribes, and I know they're still here. Trina and I have both seen them beyond the garden area. Over the last several months this evil thing has been attacking me. It's been throwing things, waking me up by poking me, trying to pull me out of bed."

Sara opened herself up to the other side and felt several presences. "There are several earthbound souls here as well as a demonic. We need to take care of the demon first, once it is gone the others will be free to leave. As for the lizard person, it is a Native American; he was a shaman whose animal was a lizard. He took on the guise of a lizard person to scare away the bad spirits and protect you and your mother. Unfortunately, he is not strong enough to defeat the demon. The Native Americans you feel and hear down by the creek are also trying to warn and protect you from it. Do you have Native American ancestry?"

"My mother was part Pueblo Indian. That's cool; I always wondered if the Indians were trying to help, but I didn't know the lizard guy was trying to protect us too."

"We will have to deal with the demonic first, and then the others will be free to leave. I want to give you a little background on myself, so you can understand how I work. Twenty years ago, I was in a motorcycle accident twenty-seven years ago. I was clinically dead for two minutes, during that time I crossed to the other side and made to relive all my lives back to what they call the core soul. I made the connection with my core soul which belongs to an archangel named Auriel. Whenever a demonic is present her consciousness comes forward to do battle with it, and my consciousness retreats. I must warn you she can be a bit abrasive and condescending towards mortals. Just know that it's not me acting that way and just ignore her attitude. I am working on her attitude, but it is a work in progress." Sara explained.

"Okay, thanks for letting us know. What if this thing tries to attack us?" Trina asked nervously.

"Not to worry I work closely with Michael the Archangel, he protects everyone while Auriel does the removal and sometimes it's the other way around." She reassured them. "Are you ready to begin?"

Trina and Tyler looked at each other and nodded ascent.

Standing up Tyler led the way to the front door of the small house. Taking a deep breath, he opened the door and stepped inside.

Lebanon Demon

Once he opened the door the full force of the negative energy hit Sara, and the surrounding air felt heavy and oppressive. She could feel Auriel stirring inside of her wanting to come forward. Suddenly the demon appeared at the far end of the room.

Sayetta and Gabe stood in the open doorway watching the events unfold.

"Oh wow, so that's what a demon looks like," Gabe said in awe.

Sayetta grinned at him, "You have to understand that everyone sees demons differently. Most of the time they will draw from your mind the image of what you think they look like and show themselves like that. If they can't find an image, they will search your mind to find your deepest fear and use that to represent themselves. Because you are with me, you see it in its true form."

"It looks different than I had envisioned. I always imagined they would be ugly, have red glowing eyes and horns, but they are amazing in a dark way. Overall, they have the appearance of a black angel until you look at their face. It's their face that seems to reflect the inner darkness within it."

"Yes, I have always thought that myself. It's a pity they cannot be reasoned with or returned to the light, but they have made their decision." She said. Shrugging she turned back to observe how Sara handled the dark entity.

"It's standing over there," Sara said pointing to the hallway leading to what she assumed was the bedrooms. "You might want to go outside or stand behind me." She told Tyler and Trina never taking her eyes off the entity.

"We'll wait by the door," Tyler told her, backing towards the door.

Sayetta and Gabe moved farther into the room and off to the side to better observe what was about to happen.

"I'm going to let you hear the conversation taking place between Sara and the demon as she does all of the work telepathically." She told him. Placing her hand on his forehead, he suddenly heard a low guttural growl from the creature standing in front of Sara.

"Bitch of a mortal creature, you can do nothing, you are no more than an irritant to me." He heard the demon growl at her.

"I always knew demons were stupid but I've never met one as dumb as you. You know nothing of me, you see what you wish to see and nothing more, like a lot of humans you judge too quickly. I see you in your true form, how many others can see your true form, just think about that for a minute or two or are you that stupid?"

"I see nothing more than a pathetic mortal who thinks she can fool me into thinking she is something more than she is. I have met your kind before, and they were never the same after I finished with them. You were foolish to come here and challenge me. Now you will pay for your foolishness." It growled at her.

"You can't scare me, you're the one who should be afraid!" she said laughing. Her laughter seemed to infuriate it all the more. "Enough," She shouted. "I am through with all your posturing and foulness it's time to send you back where you belong!"

"You can try, but you will fail. You are not the first mortal who thought to banish me. They come in with their sage and incense, saying prayers to try to cover up their lack of faith. But I see through to their weaknesses; you are no different than the others. I have enjoyed tormenting humans for many of your centuries, and I am not about to stop!"

"Really? I wouldn't be too sure about that."

Gabe moved closer so that he was able to see both the demons and Sara's face clearly.

"Auriel is coming forward," Sayetta told him.

"How can you tell?"

"I can feel Sara's consciousness shifting. Watch her face closely, and you will see the moment the transformation is complete." She instructed him.

He focused more intently on the interaction between the two in front of him.

"Foul creature, how many more of you must I send back into the darkness? Have you learned nothing over the centuries in darkness? Azuriel was right; you will never learn from your mistakes. I don't know how he can stand to be near any of you!"

"What do you know of the 'one who waits'?"

"He was my mentor." She answered, but it was not Sara who answered, but Auriel.

As Gabe watched Sara's face, voice and demeanor all changed. Her eyes were white, and her face transformed so that there was little resemblance to Sara's face.

"Know you not who I am evil one?"

"No, it's not possible, you do not take physical form!" It screeched. The sound was heard by everyone including the humans by the door.

"I have been summoned because you have been causing problems and keeping souls from ascending into the light and that I will not tolerate."

"I will not go back into the darkness; I was summoned by a human who opened a portal. If they were stupid enough to invite me into their world who am I to refuse."

"You made your choice long ago when you stood against the creator. The darkness awaits your arrival, and Azuriel is aware of your return."

As Gabe watched, Auriel put out her hands and a ball of light formed between them. With a small movement of her wrist, the ball shot from her hands and encompassed the demon.

"Noooooooo." It screamed from inside the globe.

"Be silent, nothing and no one can help you. Be thankful that the creator has shown you mercy; I would not. I defer to his judgment." She said looking disappointed in not being able to destroy it.

"The old one is coming for you, and he'll find you. Sending me back will enable him to find you." the demon warned.

"Do you think I fear any of you? He can come, and maybe I will let him live." She laughed in joyous abandon. Raising her right hand, she made a sweeping downward motion and the globe, and the demon vanished.

Gabe noticed that the moment the globe vanished Sara's face returned to normal.

As Sara turned around to address Tyler and Trina, she noticed the look on their faces. They looked stunned, horrified and relieved all at the same time.

"Let's sit down; I have a few things that you'll need to do now. The demon is gone, and it won't be back anytime soon. Your mother is now free to ascend into the light and the Native Americans who were trying to protect you can rest easy."

"What about the lizard man?" Trina asked.

"He is no longer needed to protect you; he will move on to help another person. There are a couple of things you need to do right away. First, you will need to do a white light cleansing. I have written out the instructions down for you. Both of you should do it as soon as possible. I've brought you some black salt; it is used for protection against negative entities. I was given the recipe by God when I started removing negatives. It is used to protect those who are being attacked." Digging into her backpack, she produced a jar of black salt and paper.

"Here is the salt," she said handing Tyler the jar. "Here are the instructions for the white light cleansing and the laying down of the black salt. When you are touched by the darkness like you both have been, there is residual negative energy left behind. This negative energy needs to be cleared from your body, mind, and spirit. If it's not cleared, you can attract other negative entities."

"Don't worry we're going to do it right after you leave, neither one of us want to go through that again," Tyler assured her.

"This is the first time I've seen the demon with my own eyes. Before this, all I've ever gotten is the feeling it was there and an impression of darkness. It was so terrifying to look at; I don't know how you can deal with them." Trina said visible shuttering.

"Everyone will see a demon differently. They look into your mind and draw from it what your preconceived image of what you think they should look like and what you most fear. Then they come up with something sure to frighten you to death. It's one of their most successful tricks, along with showing themselves as a child or someone you know."

"Make certain you sage before you lay down the black salt otherwise you may trap all that residual energy in the house, and that won't be very comfortable." Pulling one of her cards out of the backpack she handed it to them. "If you have any questions or something should come up give me a call, but things should be fine now." Gathering up her things she headed for the door.

Gabe and Sayetta followed them out the door and started towards where Gabe had left his car.

"That was incredible; I don't know if I'll ever be the same again." He said shaking his head.

"You say the same sort of thing in every lifetime you're with me." She told him laughing. "It is something that few mortals have ever seen or would wish to see."

"I agree few people would have the stomach for it and I think it would haunt them for the rest of their lives. I know for me it's added a whole new perspective on the darker side of the paranormal."

Arriving at the car Sayetta uncloaked them, the dogs welcomed them with a wiggle and a soft mooing sound. After petting the dogs, Sayetta told Sara telepathically to head to the park they had seen on their way to the house.

"Sara is going to meet us at the little park we passed so the dogs can get out and stretch."

"Okay," Gabe put the car in gear and flipped a U-turn heading back the way they had come. Pulling into the park's parking lot Gabe opened the back door and let the dogs out to run in the park.

A few minutes later Sara pulled into the parking lot, parking next to Gabe's car.

"How are you?" Gabe asked her.

"Fine, it's always a little draining when I do one of these. I always think, 'why are you so drained, Auriel does most of the work,' but it doesn't seem to matter." She sighed.

"It's because all of that energy is being put forth to trap the demon and of course it pushes back. Which makes it even more exhausting." Sayetta explained to her. "We're going to follow you to your place, and then we'll need to tell you the rest of the information we have."

"That sounds good. You know when you two were cloaked I couldn't sense or feel you, that's awesome." She said grinning at them, "Wish I could do that sometimes."

"Sorry, but you'd have to be dead to be able to do that little trick," Sayetta told her.

"That figures, all the good stuff isn't until you vacate the body." She said with a touch of disappointment in her voice.

Gabe brought out the dog's water and food bowls, letting them eat while Sayetta talked with Sara. After they had finished eating, Gabe picked up the bowls and placed them back in the car letting the dogs play for a few minutes. Opening the back door, he called to the dogs, and they hopped into the backseat.

"Are you ready to go Sara?" He asked.

"Yes, I'm more than ready to head for home. I'll try not to drive too fast, but I can't promise anything. My friends all call me Mario! It's probably why they bought me a visor clip the says 'never drive faster than your angels can fly'." She said, and they all laughed.

"I'm sure I can keep up, I have a rather heavy foot on the gas pedal," Gabe assured her climbing into the car.

Sara climbed behind the wheel of her car and started the engine.

Sanctuary

They spent the next hour and a half making their way to Sara's farm. They pulled off the main road and onto a finely graveled road, which turned out to be a mile-long driveway. The driveway was flanked on both sides by corrals where cattle, sheep, and llamas grazed contentedly. At the end of the driveway was a huge house which was a mixture of Dutch colonial and plantation style. A large garage stood apart from the house as they approached the house Sara triggered the garage door opener. Sara pulled her car inside next to a black motorcycle and a newer pickup truck.

Gabe pulled up in front of the garage just as Sara was got out of the car.

"You can go ahead and bring the dogs through this gate. I have a fenced in backyard, and they can run and play in the yard." she said heading towards the small gate at the side of the house.

Clipping the leash on the dogs, he followed Sayetta and Sara into the yard. Once inside the yard, he took off their leashes, and they began to run and play.

Sara unlocked the side door of the house and was greeted by three sets of eager doggy eyes. "Alright, you three I've brought some friends to visit. Yes, go ahead outside and meet them," she told the dogs. She opened the door fully to allow the dogs to go outside.

Gabe and Sayetta watched as two Dobermans and a springer spaniel pushed past them.

"Come on in and, there is ice tea, ice water and fresh lemon aide in the fridge help yourself. There are some bowls in the cupboard next to the fridge for ice water for your dogs." Opening the French doors located off the backyard patio, she motioned them to follow her outside. "Let me introduce you to my four legged children. The large Doberman is Zeus, and the smaller one is Jenny. This girl," she said rubbing the ears on the black and white springer spaniel "is Susie. Why don't you guys just relax at the kitchen table for a while and I'll show you around after I check my answering machine." Sara said heading into the house.

"I don't know about you, but I could use some ice tea. Would you like some ice water?" Gabe asked.

"Yes, that sounds good, it is getting warmer." Sayetta agreed.

They could hear Sara in the distance listening to her messages.

Gabe found a large bowl put some ice in it and filled it with water. He grabbed a couple of glasses and filled them, handing Sayetta her water.

"I think I'll go outside and check on the dogs." She told him picking up the bowl and heading towards the door.

"Okay, I want to get my laptop and check emails." He told her following her out the door.

As they stepped outside the dogs were running and playing. Sayetta called them telepathically to her and led them towards the stone patio area by the French doors. An oval glass table with padded lounge chairs was located at the far end of the patio. She put the ice water bowl down on the patio, and the dogs began slurping it down. Smiling, she sat down at the table and watched the dogs as the ran off to play.

Gabe found her there relaxing and joined her at the table sitting down he opened the laptop and turned it on. He noticed a small bar next to the French doors. "I wonder if she keeps some ice in the bar." He said to himself.

Walking over to the bar, he found a small refrigerator with an ice dispenser on the back side of it. Taking a glass out of the bar, he filled it with ice and poured it into the dog's water bowl. Sitting down at the table, he began reading his mail.

Sara opened the patio door a few minutes later and joined them. They sat in comfortable silence for a few minutes enjoying the antics of the dogs.

"Sara, I need to tell you something that Auriel is not going to like so be prepared."

"Michael, can you join us?" She asked telepathically. "I've asked Michael to join us." She told Gabe, knowing full well that Auriel would have heard her telepathic message to Michael.

Michael appeared standing next to Sayetta. Using his new-found abilities, Gabe focused on hearing and seeing Michael. Like an autofocus on a camera, the image of Michael appeared before him and slowly became clear. He could hear his deep melodious voice speaking. As he appeared, the dogs ceased their antics and ran over to greet him. He took the time to pet each one of them before turning his attention to the others.

"Sayetta, Gabe good to see you again. Looking at Sara, he nodded to something that only they could hear.

"I have asked Michael to be here in case Auriel gets too upset by my news. Only he can restrain her." Sayetta told him softly.

"I wondered if it might be something like that. It's a wise precaution." He agreed.

"Alright Sayetta, whenever you're ready," Michael told her.

"Sara, I want to give you a little background on the incident that happened several hundred years ago. There was an old demon who was given a task by Lucifer which he failed to accomplish. He was given the assignment of turning Paul against Jesus. He failed in his task. It actually backfired on him. Instead of it weakening his faith it strengthened his faith in Jesus. When the creator heard, what had happened he was enraged and sent Auriel to deal with the demon. Auriel was forced to return him to the darkness when all she wanted to do was to eradicate him from existence. In his infinite wisdom, the creator knew that destroying the creature would be too swift a death for it. He knew that anything he could do to it would be nothing compared to what Lucifer would do. So, He had Auriel send it back into the darkness knowing full well that Lucifer does not tolerate failure. In his anger, Lucifer didn't care that Demicides was one of his best soldiers and imprisoned him in the earth."

Sara could feel Auriel stirring at the mention of the demon's name coming forward.

Gabe had been watching Sara closely and noticed the change in her demeanor as Auriel came forward. Unlike the other time when there was a demon present, there was no physical change in Sara, except for the color of her eyes and the change in her voice.

"So, Lucifer has released his prisoner, very interesting." Auriel mused.

"He has sent him to kill not only your physical body but your soul consciousness as well," Sayetta told her.

"Lucifer doesn't strike me as being particularly stupid, I would say more like delusional. He's probably thinking there might be an off chance that Demicides would succeed and if he does than Michael will take him out, thereby getting rid of two thorns in his side. I think he overestimates his minion's abilities. I'm surprised that he would take Lucifer up on his offer, he must either be desperate or had no choice in the matter. Now that I think about it Lucifer would not have given him a choice." Auriel reasoned.

"Exactly my thought," Sayetta told her.

"How did you find out he was being sent to find me?" Auriel wanted to know.

"Azuriel was given the information by one of the lesser minions who was seeking a return to the light," Michael told her. "He knew he dared not come himself, so he charged one of his angels to contact a medium that was known to Gabe."

"Michael, did you know about this?" Auriel asked him.

"I only knew something negative was coming, but I swear to you I didn't know who it was." He assured her. "Would you like me to deal with him for you?"

Michael knew the moment the words left his mouth that he had made a mistake in uttering them. But the need to protect her was too great for him not to offer. He braced himself for the anger and indignation he was sure would come.

"Thank you, Michael, for offering, but you know this is something that I have to deal with myself." she told him quietly.

Michael was aware of her anger, but it was not directed at him for asking. Normally she would have exploded as she had in the past if someone tried to help. He could tell she had her anger under tight control. He had taken her aside about a year ago, and let her know the anger and disdain she had for the humans was causing Sara problems in the physical world. Her attitude was being projected through Sara causing others in her circle to think she was arrogant. Auriel didn't care what the other humans thought, but she didn't want to disappoint the creator. If she could not do her job, she would be letting the creator down. He could see she had taken to heart their earlier discussion.

"Gabriel and I will be monitoring the situation. I believe that the last removal has given him the information he needs to find you. Sara, be mindful of your surroundings and be very careful once you leave your protected farm." Michael warned.

Auriel's consciousness receded, and Sara's was again dominant. "I'll be careful Michael don't you worry and with Sayetta and Gabe here there will be extra eyes to keep watch."

Gabriel suddenly appeared beside Sayetta. "I have taken the liberty of increasing Titus and Lucy's sensitivity to not only light beings but also the darker ones. They will be able to sound the alarm when they sense a negative presence."

"Thank both of you for your help in this matter. Michael, you've worked with Sara how would you say her training is coming?"

"She is only using about three-quarters of her abilities right now. I have been able to help her tap into Auriel's powers and use them here in the physical world." He told her.

Turning to Sara, Sayetta said, "I will need to gauge the extent of your abilities by making the connection with you and open you up the rest of the way. I thought we could do it tonight."

Gabe winced at Sayetta's assumption that Sara didn't have anything better to do tonight.

Seeing the look on Gabe's face, Sara told him. "Gabe, it's okay, being with Michael all this time I'm used to the archangel's way of doing things."

"I am truly sorry; Sara I did not mean it to sound like an order. Please check your schedule and let me know if it is convenient for you. Sometimes I am not aware of how humans perceive my words. That is why Gabe is always sent ahead of me so that he can help guide me in the physical world." Sayetta informed her.

"Believe me I am well acquainted with Michael's bossy ways," Sara said giving Michael a knowing look.

"Hey I take exception to that, I am not bossy as you put it. I just know what's right for you better than you do." He told her looking affronted that she should think of him as bossy.

"No, I have nothing pressing so far as I know. I usually spend my evenings writing and answering my emails and messages. I'm flexible and can do those things in the morning and do my writing later." Sara told Sayetta.

"That will be fine; we can do it after dinner," Sayetta asked.

"I usually eat dinner around five. I have to feel the animals one more time before bed."

"Fine, I will help you feed the animals in the morning so that I can learn the routine, then I will be able to feed them in the morning before you get up. I do not require sleep but rather keep in touch with Ezekiel and catch up on the events on the other side. I tried to sleep the other night I found it revitalizing for the physical body but the sensation unsettling to me."

"Let's go inside, and I'll show you where you're going to sleep, then we'll get dinner started."

Opening the French door, they passed through the kitchen it was a huge kitchen done in varying shades of blue. Stainless steel appliances arranged in strategic area's around the kitchen for prep work. Leaving the kitchen, through an open doorway brought you into in to the dining room which was small and formal looking. On the other side of it was the living room.

"This is my favorite lounging spot in the house. It's comfortable; there is a big screen TV and entertainment system. The dogs and I watch movies together." She confided to them. Just off the living room was the east wing of the house.

"The guest bedrooms are in this wing of the house; it affords my guests privacy. Here are the two rooms you can use." Sara said motioning to two bedrooms, one on each side of the hallway. At the end of the hallway was a large sitting area with a television, computer desk, and comfortable, easy chairs.

"Gabe this is where you can use your computer. I have secure wireless access, and you'll need to enter the password get access. The password is demonseer, all one word."

"Sayetta you can use the other room for some privacy. I also have a meditation room that I know you will feel right at home in. Follow me, and I'll show you."

Turning around, they retraced their steps out of the guest wing. They followed Sara and entered the foyer where a grand staircase led upstairs. As they approached the upstairs landing, Sayetta could feel a change in the energy. The energy felt like the divine had touched it.

Gabe also felt the change in the energy, it felt warm and comforting and reminded him of Gabriel.

Sara stopped on the landing to give them time to feel the change that she knew they were feeling. She looked at Sayetta and saw a warm smile fill her face. Gabe had a sort of mystified look on his face, ever the thinker she could tell he was trying to make sense of what he was feeling.

"May I?" Sayetta asked her.

"Of course, please feel free," Sara told her.

"I think I'll tag along with Sayetta as she seems to know where she's going," Gabe said grinning at Sara.

Sayetta headed down the hallway not bothering to look into the open doors as she passed. She seemed intent on getting to the end of the long hallway where a stained-glass door sat closed. As he followed her he could feel himself being drawn to the same door at the end of the hall; he experienced a feeling of coming home. The sensation was strange for him as he had never been here before.

Sayetta had reached the door and ran her hand lovingly over the stained glass which depicted clouds with white light rays emanating from it lighting a set of stairs leading into the clouds. It was one on the most beautiful stained-glass doors he had ever seen.

Turning to look at him her face was lit with an unearthly glow. "Can you feel what lies beyond this door?" she asked him.

Seeing the bewilderment on his face, she smiled serenely, "A little piece of heaven." she told him.

He didn't understand what she was trying say. She pushed open the door and entered the room. As the door opened, he was hit by a wave of pure white light energy. He could feel his senses reeling from it and had to steady himself against the door frame to keep from falling over. Once he could think again, he opened his senses and could feel some sort of doorway or portal.

As he entered the room, the energy decreased enough so that his dizziness was manageable. Looking around the room he realized this was a place of great power. Statues and pictures of archangels filled the room. Closing his eyes, he concentrated on seeing what could not be seen with the naked eye. Slowly opening his eyes, he could see a vortex of energy right in the middle of the room, and Sayetta was standing right in the middle of it. Her image seemed to waver in and out of focus.

"What you are seeing is an archangel with one foot in the physical world and the other in the angelic plane. It's an exhilarating feeling standing in the middle of it; you should try it." Sara told him.

"I don't know whether I'm already for that. I'm already experiencing dizziness just being in the room."

"Gabe, take my hand," Sayetta called out holding her hand out for him to take.

Slowly he reached for her outstretched hand. They moment their hands touched he felt the energy enter his body. He could sense his physical consciousness slipping away and in its place, another stronger consciousness emerging. He was no longer bound by his physical body. Instead, he had the sense of what he assumed was an astral body. Looking down at his hands, he could see they were translucent.

"This is who you are, Zebulon warrior angel," Sayetta told him.

He felt free, powerful yet gentle and above all loved. He could fell millions of other souls surrounding him, and then he felt the creator. He could feel the creator telling him how proud he was of him. It was an empowering feeling but one he knew he had to leave it behind and return to his body. In a millisecond, he was back in his physical body. He stepped out of the vortex leaving Sayetta standing in the middle.

After a few minutes, Sayetta left the vortex smiling serenely. "It's always good to call home as you say. You're right Sara; it's the perfect place to meditate."

"I knew you'd feel right at home here. Michael opened a small portal so Auriel could feel closer to home. When I meditate, she talks to them and directs the healing of people who have come to me asking for healing. I don't think I told you the creator had given me the gift of healing? If I can touch the person it works faster, if not I do it through meditation from a distance."

"I am glad the creator has found outlets for Auriel. I now see that if she didn't have some outlets for her power, it would be hard to contain her within a physical body." Sayetta reasoned.

"Come on, I'll fix us some dinner, and you can unload your things from the car. I'll take care of the dogs." She told them leading them back towards the kitchen.

Gabe and Sayetta headed out to the car to gather their belongings and bring them in.

"Gabe, something negative and powerful is nearby," Sayetta said stopping next to the car.

"Can you tell what it is?"

"I think it maybe Demicides, he's getting closer."

"How close is close?"

She closed her eyes and opened her senses. "Maybe 50 to 60 miles from here."

"Let's get back inside."

Gathering their belongings, they headed back into the house. Once inside they headed for the sitting room next to his bedroom. He put his equipment including his computer on the table. They made another trip out to the car to get his suitcase and the dog things. He put Titus's bed in his bedroom and Lucy's bed in Sayetta's room. Once everything was arranged, they headed back towards the kitchen. They found Sara placing the food on the table.

"Does someone want to feed the dogs?" She asked them.

"I'll do it," Sayetta told her.

Sara pulled a large container from the second refrigerator by the door. "I don't like feeding my dogs bagged dog food; they put too many preservatives and other things in it. This is a mixture of meat, rice, and vegetables which I cook weekly. Here's a scoop you can use to put the food in the bowls. Two scoops in each bowl should be about right. We'll feed them outside that way if they make a mess it doesn't matter. I do have a maintenance man who comes in to take care of the grounds and a housekeeper that comes in three days a week."

Sara pulled out a large tray and placed the bowls of dog food on it.

"Gabe, can you open the door and let the dogs outside please?" Sara asked him.

Opening the door, the dogs all ran outside followed closely by Sayetta with a tray full of dog food. Setting the tray on the table, she told the dogs to sit down and handed each one of them their bowl of food. Picking up the tray, she reentered the house.

"I've made a fresh salad, baked chicken and fresh fruit for dessert. I made these rolls fresh yesterday." Sara told them handing Gabe a basket of them. They all sat down at the table, offered a prayer and ate in silence.

Finishing their dinner, Sayetta was the first to speak. She looked at Sara and said, "He's close, very close I can feel him."

"I know I can feel him too. Fortunately for us, he doesn't know exactly where we are."

A Cry for Help

Getting up Sara began to clear the table. Sayetta helped her finish clearing the table and putting the food away.

"Well if you don't need my help I'm going to check my emails and do a little writing," Gabe told them.

"After I finish here I'm going to do little of the same," Sara told him letting the dogs back in the house.

As Gabe got up, Titus came running to him, following him out of the room. Lucy and the other two dogs stayed in the kitchen with Sara and Sayetta.

"If you're ready I'll open you up the rest of the way. Please sit down, and we'll get started." Sayetta said motioning to her recently vacated kitchen chair.

Sara sat down, closed her eyes and felt Sayetta place her hands on either side of her head. Immediately she felt a white light explosion fill her head. The power of it made her dizzy and left her feeling breathless. She felt her remove her hands and the explosion stopped

"How do you feel?" Sayetta asked.

"Strange but in a good way, the only word I use to describe it is enlightened."

"Yes, that suits." Sayetta agreed.

Glancing at Sayetta, Sara knew where she wanted to be right then. "Why don't you go up to the meditation room for little peace and quiet. I'm going to be in my office if you need anything just holler."

Sayetta smiled and told Lucy telepathically to find Gabe and Titus and stay with them. Lucy got up and followed her nose to find Titus. She found both of them in the sitting room and lay down next to Titus.

Sayetta headed upstairs to the meditation room and closed the door entering the vortex. Meanwhile, Sara entered her office with the dogs following closely behind her. Turning her computer on she stretched and grabbed an ice water out of the small refrigerator in the corner of her office. Sitting down at the computer, Sara paid her accounts and checked her email. Just as she was about to shut the computer down the Facebook messenger icon popped up notifying her of a message. She hesitated for a moment then clicked on the icon.

The first line read: 'Please help me' in large capital letters. She quickly opened the message, and a wave of evil hit her so hard it nearly took her breath away. It had been a long time since she had felt anything that overwhelmingly negative. She could feel Auriel coming to the forefront of her consciousness. *'Read the rest of the message; I sense an old one.'* She heard her say. The message read:

'Please help us; we are being terrorized nightly by some evil presence. It is slapping, scratching, punching our children. My husband and I are having nightmares, being pulled out of bed and something is choking us in our sleep. We have been unable to find anyone to help us you are our last resort. We cannot afford to move but we cannot stay in the house either, we will be homeless.' At the end of the message was a phone number.

By the time, she had finished reading the message she was shaking. Auriel was right she could feel the evil presence. It was so strong that it made her sick to her stomach.

Opening her mind, she reached out towards the sender of the message and picked up on several things, none of which were good occurring in the house. The first thing she picked up on was the fear and terror of the people living in the home. The next thing she picked up on was the minions and one lesser demon. The final impression was on something much stronger and more evil lurking in the background. The evil emanating from it set her teeth on edge, and her skin crawl.

Glancing at the clock, she realized it was too late in the evening to contact the woman who sent the message came. She would call her first thing in the morning, for now, she would get some more writing done.

Three hours later she finished writing three chapters and realized it was getting late. "Alright, you two let's get you outside to do your duty then it's off to bed."

Sara woke early the next morning, took a shower and got dressed. The dogs followed closely behind her as she headed for the kitchen to put a pot of coffee on. After starting the coffee, she noticed that Titus and Lucy were already outside. Opening the door, she let her dogs out and headed for the barn to feed the animals. Arriving at the barn, she saw Sayetta sitting on the corral fence watching the animals. She should have known she would be up early; she probably didn't sleep much if at all.

"Good morning Sara." She heard her say telepathically.

"Good morning," she responded in kind. "How long have you been out here?"

"I came out when the first golden rays of the sun warmed the earth."

Sara laughed, "A woman after my own heart. I'm usually up and out here about then but having company throws me off. That and writing for three hours last night. I've put some coffee on; I get the impression that Gabe usually has a couple of cups in the morning. He's a writer, too isn't he?"

"Yes, he uses what he calls a pen name. I believe it's Gabriel West or something like that."

"Well I've certainly heard of him, he writes those fictional paranormal investigator stories. I read one of them a while back; it seems like I never have time anymore to do much reading." Sara said with a sigh.

"I've fed everyone this morning, and I put the fresh eggs I gathered in the refrigerator for you."

"Let's have breakfast on the patio. Why don't you see if Gabe's up and about yet? If he is, tell him, I'm making breakfast, and if he doesn't come down soon, I can't guarantee there will be any coffee left." She told her as they arrived back at the house.

The Trap

Demicides decided that he needed a little help in locating Auriel, so he summoned Jonti one of his minions.

"Master I'm here at your service."

"I need you to do a little scouting for me. I am seeking an archangel in human form, and it is within your vicinity. I want you to draw her out so that I might destroy her."

"An archangel you say? But they only ever take human form for but a brief moment. Why is she here and how will I find her?" He questioned.

"Be silent." Demicides snarled at him. "Did you not hear me? I said she is in human form, surely you've heard about our brother who was entombed in the earth who was released recently?"

"Oh, yes master, I heard a rumor, but I didn't believe it to be true. Are you saying it is indeed true?"

"Yes, upon his return Lucifer destroyed him for not killing the one who sent him back. Lucifer is very upset about it. This archangel was reborn into human form and must be destroyed."

"But master I cannot kill an archangel, I would surely either be destroyed or returned to the dark realm," Jonti told him a look of absolute terror on his face.

"Be calm, all I ask is that you lure her out of her protective place and I will do the rest." He said smiling evilly at the minion.

Jonti did not like the look of the smile on his face. He had heard about the old ones using their minions to lure out an angel. Ninety percent of the time the minion was returned to the darkness, and he didn't want to go back. He had purposely kept a low profile in the physical world, only causing minor disturbances so as not to draw attention to himself. Here was his master asking him to piss off an archangel. He knew where there was one; there would be others close by. He had to think of a plan to lure her out without sacrificing himself. He didn't care what his master wanted; he was not going to go up against an archangel alone.

"Which one of the archangels is it?" he asked.

"What does it matter, you dare to question me?" Demicides shouted.

"But master, it will make it easier for me if I know which one it is, they all have their quirks." He whined.

Demicides thought about it for a moment and decided that it sounded reasonable. "Auriel, its Auriel." He enjoyed seeing the look of fear on the minion's face.

Jonti cringed when he heard the name. This archangel was the one who disarmed Lucifer's son during the battle between the light and darkness. Then a thought occurred to him, what if he were able to turn the tables on his master? A plan started forming in his mind.

He knew exactly what to do. A short while ago he had been tormenting a family until they were so terrified that they moved. A new family had moved in, and so far he had been watching them and did little things to unsettle them. He figured he could ramp up the activity and put the thought into their head to find a local demonologist. That should do the trick as long as they get a hold of her, he would see to it that they did. Then all he had to do it tell his master where to find her and leave them to it. Feeling extremely pleased with himself he told his master.

"Don't worry master; I have a plan to draw her out. I'll let you know when and where."

"Jonti, don't screw this up or you will feel Lucifer's wrath." He warned him.

"No master, I won't" He assured him getting as far away from him as he could.

Demicides was not impressed with Jonti. He had been on the physical plane too long, and he had not received any reports of his activities in a long time. He wondered if he had grown too fond of the physical world. He decided it might be a good idea if he kept an eye on him when this was over.

Jonti, on the other hand, knew his master was not someone who you could trust or show any weakness. He had to be very careful not to say anything to anyone, not even his minions. He would start ramping up his activity tonight. He knew that if you targeted the children in the house, it would ensure that the parents would act quickly.

In the next moment darkness, had fallen and it was time for him to go to work. He spent the night opening and closing closet doors, pulling the blankets off of the children and making them scream. Once they were settled down, he headed to the parents' bedroom. Climbing on top of the woman he started choking her until she almost lost consciousness. Choking and coughing she tried to call out her husband's name but was only able to get out a whisper. The next thing she knew her husband was being pulled out of bed by his feet. Startled he tried to stop himself from being pulled out of the bed but was unable to landing on the floor with a thud.

He couldn't resist one last parting shot in the form of three scratches down the man's back. '*There,*' he thought to himself, '*if that doesn't do it nothing will. Now all he has to do is get them to look online for a demonologist.*'

The next morning, he had the woman do was get online to search for someone to help them.

"Go online and search for a demonologist in your area" He instructed the woman telepathically. Three hours later and they were no closer to finding a reputable one. He had no idea that it would be so difficult for them to find one. For the next two days, the humans searched online. The humans were growing desperate, and he was growing frustrated because they weren't making any headway in finding her. Finally, he decided that he would have them try a different route. He had spent almost a hundred years watching these humans, and in the last twenty years, he noticed that they seemed to spend a lot of time on something called social networking. Maybe that was the way for them to find her.

"Look on your social media sites and see what you can find." He advised the man telepathically.

"Why don't we try Facebook and see what we can find." The man told his wife.

"Good idea maybe a paranormal group or something."

A couple of hours later they found a name, Sara Lion.

"Pull up her picture," Jonti told them.

The woman clicked on the picture of the woman, and Jonti staggered back in fright. Staring back at him was the image of Auriel, even though it was only a picture her power came through. The thought of having to deal with her sent shivers through him. She had no patience or love for his kind, hell she had no love for anyone but her kind. Let Demicides go up against her because he certainly wasn't going to risk himself.

"Let's send her a message and see if she's willing to help us." The woman suggested.

"Good idea, let's hope she answers soon. Because if we don't get some help we'll have to abandon the house all together and I don't know where we would go." The man said sounding desperate.

The woman explained her situation in the message and put in their phone number. Pushing the enter key with extra force, she said a silent prayer for help.

Jonti cringed at the prayer but hoped she'd take the bait. Now all he had to do was sit back and wait for the response. Knowing that things always seemed to take forever in the physical world, he decided to use his minions to keep up the activity while he scouted out another person to terrorize. He knew that once Auriel was here, he could never return to this house even if he wanted to. Summoning his minions, he gave them their orders and told them to report immediately if the humans heard back from the archangel. Most of his minions were loyal to him, but even some of them wanted to leave once they found out that an archangel was coming.

Making the Connection

With a groan, Gabe rolled out of bed and realized that he had slept in, it was just after 6 am and he was usually up by 5:30. No wonder he was late getting up, Titus wasn't in his bed. He was always good at getting him up on time. Taking a quick shower, he finished dressing and opened his door to find Sayetta waiting.

"Sara said to tell you if you don't come down soon there won't be any coffee left." She said grinning at him.

"Now that would be a fate worse than death." He responded grinning back. He could smell bacon. Fresh toast and coffee. He could only hope there were eggs to go with no the bacon.

They headed for the kitchen and arrived just in time to see Sara finish feeding the dogs out on the patio. Stepping through the patio door, Sara smiled and asked Gabe, "Ready for some coffee?"

"I'm never fully awake until I have at least 2 cups."

Reaching up into the cabinet, Sara pulled out a couple of cups and filled them both. "There's cream in the fridge and sugar in the bowl." She told him pulling the sugar bowl out of the cupboard.

"Breakfast is done, Gabe, will you grab some plates, there in the cupboard next to the coffee pot.

"Sayetta there's a bowl of fruit in the fridge, can you set it on the table?" She asked gathering napkins and silverware.

Sayetta took the fruit out of the refrigerator set it on the table and poured herself a glass of ice tea.

They all sat down, said a prayer and the conversation turned general.

"So, what is everyone doing today?" Sara asked.

"I thought I'd do a little writing then go for a walk around your place, visit the animals and soak up the atmosphere," Gabe said.

"I need to check in with the creator and give him an update one what is happening."

"I'm going to update my website. Why don't you take the dogs with you on your walk Gabe? They know not to go beyond the protective line and so do yours now."

"Sure, I can do that, I think they'll be glad for the excuse to run loose."

Finishing breakfast, they all helped clear off the table, putting things away and putting the dishes in the dishwasher.

"If you'll excuse me I'm going to leave now; I'll be back soon," Sayetta told them and disappeared.

"Well that was unsettling, I've never seen her do that before, it creeped me out," Gabe said.

"Don't worry about it, you'll get used to it after a while, I did," Sara told him and headed for her office.

Gabe didn't think he would ever get used to something like that. Shrugging off the feeling, he headed for the sitting room to get some writing done.

Thinking about the message she received last night she knew she needed to help these people; there was no question of that. The entity was too powerful to be a lesser demon or a minion. She would have to speak to Gabe and Sayetta about this. She was sure without question that there was an old demon somewhere in the mix.

There was only one way to know for certain if what she was picking up was accurate or not; she would have to make the connection through a phone call. Taking a deep breath, she picked up the phone and dialed the number. It rang several times before it was picked up by a woman with a quiver in her voice.

"Hello?"

"Hello, this is Sara."

"Oh, thank God, thank God!" The woman exclaimed and broke down crying.

She let her cry for a minute or two while she made use of her senses, probing the energy on the other end of the line. She could see three minions and sense a demon connected them as well as a stronger demonic presence connected to the less powerful demon.

"It's alright; I'm here to help you, can you answer a few questions?"

"Yes of course, what do you want to know?"

"Your name is Judy, right?

"Yes, Judy Spenser."

"Well Judy, how long has this been going on and did it get worse recently," Sara asked.

"At first it was just small things like hearing voices, things being moved, dishes rattling in the cupboard. Then the nightmares and the smell of sulfur started. The knocking in sets of three began. After that, the girls were scratched and slapped. Within the last two weeks, it's gotten significantly worse; we'er being physically attacked. Almost every night we are either pulled out of bed or choked."

"I think there is something more to this than just your average haunting."

"I think there's something very evil here. Are you going to help us?" Judy asked hopefully.

"Yes, I'll come this afternoon. Is there anywhere you can go for an hour?"

"I guess we can go to the park. What time do you plan to be here?"

"Where do you live?"

"We live in Molalla; I'll message you the address."

"I'll need your cell phone, so I can let you know when to return. I should be there by noon. You'll need to leave the house and leave the door unlocked or leave me a key." Sara instructed her.

"Alright, I'll leave a key in the mailbox on the front porch. Thank you, thank you so much for helping us."

Hanging up the phone, she pondered the situation for a few minutes when her cell phone chimed announcing a message had been received.

"This is it; you'll have to do battle with the old demon." Michael the archangel told her appearing before her. "This is a test for you, and it is something I cannot interfere in."

"Gee thanks, Sayetta and Gabe can come along to observe, I guess they can't help me either?"

"No, this is something that needs to be handled by Auriel, she is who he has come to destroy," Michael informed her.

"Okay, I had better tell them so they can prepare to accompany me. I also need to prepare and gather my tools for the removal." She told him getting up from her desk. The dogs followed closely behind her. Zeus whined from somewhere behind her, and the other two whined in response. Turning in response to their whining She reassured them, "Don't worry you guys nothing will happen to me except I'll be more tired than usual after the removal."

She headed towards the east wing to speak with Gabe. Arriving at the door to the sitting room, she found Gabe deep in thought, staring at his computer monitor. Knocking on the door, she entered the room.

"Hard at it, I see." She said smiling at him.

"Sara, what's up? I can tell by the look in your eyes something isn't right." He asked in concern.

"It's time, Demicides has found me." She told him.

"He sure zeroed in on you in a hurry; I thought we'd have a few days at least. How did he find you?" He asked.

"The only thing I can think of is he used one of his lesser demons or minions who are loyal to him to draw me out. I received an instant messenger request last night. The first words were 'please help me.' When I called the woman a few minutes ago, I could feel several entities in the home. There were a couple of minions and one lesser demon that was actively present, but I could sense something much eviler just out of reach."

"We had better tell Sayetta." He said feeling an overwhelming sense of anticipation and anxiety.

"I am here; there is no need for anxiety Gabe," Sayetta said appearing before them. "You both need to prepare for the upcoming encounter with prayer and white light energy. They will help to shield and protect you."

"So where are we going and when?" Gabe asked.

"There's a town called Molalla, its about 12-20 miles away, it won't take long to get there. There's a family of four being terrorized by a demon and a couple of minions. Two of the four are small children, and I cannot tolerate that. We have to be there by noon. I asked the family to leave for an hour. They've left us a key to go in and do what we need to."

"You know it's a trap, don't you?" Sayetta asked calmly.

"Yes, Auriel is well aware of the situation and is prepared to do battle," Sara told her calmly.

"How can you be so calm? You're talking about one of the most powerful demons there is!" Gabe asked.

Turning her head to look directly at him she told him, "I've defeated him before, this time will be no different."

As she spoke, he could see Auriel looking out of her eyes, and it gave him chills to see the power emanating from them. He could almost feel sorry for the demons, not! Looking at his watch, he was surprised to see that it was almost eleven. "Well we had better prepare then, I'm going to bring my equipment, demon or not I hope to get some great evidence."

"I agree I have some preparing to do myself, I have to make sure my protection is very strong and in place, before we leave." She told them and left the room.

He started gathering his investigative gear together when Sayetta said something that stopped him in his tracks.

"Gabe, we cannot help her in what she is about to do. This is something she must do alone. It is a test of faith, and we must not interfere or distract her."

"What?" he all but shouted. "You can't possibly be serious!"

"I am very serious; this is something that each of the other archangels we are looking for will have to do. Once they pass the test, it will unleash their full potential. It will open them up the rest of the way to receive the rest of their power."

"Can't Michael or Gabriel help?"

"They will be watching, but they cannot interfere unless the demon prevails, then they will destroy it."

"But that means Auriel will be destroyed!" he said incredulously sitting down heavily in a nearby chair.

"It is a chance she is willing to take to defeat it," Sayetta told him. It is a chance all we archangels take when dealing with one of the old ones."

"Well if I can't help, I'm going to document whatever I can get on film or handheld." He told her stubbornly, refusing to take no for an answer.

She did not respond, only shook her head as if she couldn't fathom why he would want to record any of it. She didn't want to tell him that it would do him no good to record, as he probably wouldn't pick up anything anyway. Oh well, it would keep him busy while Sara and Auriel were facing the demon.

Sara entered her meditation room with the dogs following close behind. They took up their usual places on either side of the energy field. She entered the vortex, opening herself up and drawing energy from the other side. She heard the voice of the creator speak to her.

"Child, be not afraid or anxious, I am with you always."

A great peace entered her, and she felt the power of the creator fill her. She stepped out of the vortex. With her dogs in tow, she headed for her office to gather the things she would need to cleanse and protect the house. Gathering together her holy water, bible, crucifix, white sage, anointing oil and black salt she placed them in her small backpack.

Turning, she found Michael standing behind her with his wings outstretched. The only time he ever did that was when he was in protection mode. "I will have your back as I always have." He said sincerely.

"I know, but this is something you cannot protect me from, it is a test I will not fail," Sara told him smiling reassuringly.

"You will face him in a physical form, unlike the last time you dealt with him."

"I understand but this form is not weak, and neither am I," Auriel assured him.

His wings slowly folded behind him. "Well then, let the games begin. Gabriel and I will have a front row seat, cloaked of course." He said grinning rubbing his hands together in anticipation, as he vanished.

Making her way to the kitchen, she put her things on the table and went into the back yard to speak with the dogs. She called them to her and told them they would only be gone for a couple of hours and they were to guard the house. She put out some food and water on the patio for them and opened one side of the French doors so she could pull out a retractable door with a built in the doggy door for them.

"That's a great door; I need to get one of them for my French doors at home," Gabe told her.

"I'll email you the information so you can have it when you get home. It's a local company that makes them." She told him.

"Shall we go?" Sayetta asked from somewhere behind them.

"Yes, well take my car." She told them. Picking up her bags she headed for the connecting door to the garage. Opening the back hatch of her soul, she loaded her things inside and motioned for Gabe to do the same.

Taking her cell phone out of her pocket, she punched in the code to open the garage door. They climbed in the vehicle, and she backed out of the garage. Once the car cleared the door, it automatically closed behind them.

They traveled in silence for several miles, each lost in his own thoughts. Gabe broke the silence asking, "How long until we arrive?"

"We should be there in another fifteen minutes. Gabe go ahead and set up your camera and place your recorder in the house in the living room when we get there. After you've got everything setup, then you'll need to stay out of the way if you insist on being there. I can't have you distracting me once we are inside. Do not speak or touch me once things start to happen."

"Right, I'll remember," Gabe told her.

"I will cloak myself so they cannot detect me. If they should attack you, Gabe, I will be unable to help you in my cloaked state." Sayetta told him. "Are you sure you want to go in with Sara?"

"I'll take my chances; it's now or never. I know that if I don't face them now, I might never have the courage to do it again." He told them.

"Very well, oh and Gabe," Sara said

"Yes?"

"Welcome to my world." She said grimly.

Just before arriving Sayetta cloaked herself and disappeared from view.

They pulled up in front of a small modern home with a fenced yard and flowers in the yard.

"You would never know by looking at it, that there's something evil inside. It looks like a typical suburban home." Gabe commented.

"As you know, looks can be deceptive," Sara said getting out of the car.

Gabe followed suit and headed for the back of the car. Opening the hatch, he grabbed his gear and looked around to find Sara staring at the house with a faraway look on her face.

"It's here, can you feel it?" She asked him.

"Yeah, it's making me sick to my stomach, and I feel cold to the very center of my being. I've never felt anything like it, and I don't want to ever again."

Battle Against Evil

"Let's get on with it then; I can already feel my adrenalin pumping, let the battle begin." She said grinning at him.

"So, you do this sort of thing a lot?" he asked nervously.

"Not on the grand scale of today's, but yes quite often. I enjoy getting rid of these things, especially when they are terrorizing children. Payback's a bitch." She said grinning.

Grabbing her things out of the car, she headed for the front porch and found the key in the mailbox as they said it would be.

Unlocking the front door, the house appeared to be quiet at first, but the air felt thick and heavy. She could feel the old one was close. It was biding its time observing the situation and just waiting for its chance to strike. The house was an open concept which helped when it came to something like this. There were fewer places for the entities to hide and you stand a better chance of seeing what was coming at you.

"Gabe, its close be careful. Are you through sitting up?" she asked him. Hyperaware she never shifted her focus off of the room in general.

"Yeah, I'm done. I'm going to move to your left to check out the kitchen." He told her moving cautiously towards the entrance to the kitchen. In the next instant, he felt something hit his chest, and he was sent flying back into the living room landing at Sara's feet.

He felt like he had been hit in the chest by a bull, it took him a moment or two to catch his breath.

"Get up, get up now!" Sara said forcefully.

He got up and headed for the far side of the living room next to the front door. Just as he reached the entry way, he heard Sara shout, "Look out!"

He was picked up and thrown across the room. It knocked the breath out of him, and it took a minute or two for him to catch his breath.

"Enough!" he heard someone say. Turning to look back towards Sara he saw her standing stone still. He needed to find out what was going on so used what Sayetta had taught him and concentrated on seeing beyond the physical plane. It took him a moment, but it all came into view. There before him stood Auriel just outside of Sara's physical body. She had such a powerful image that it blinded him for a split second.

Like Sayetta she had large, powerful wings, her face was heart shaped, and she looked like she was about 25 years old until you looked at her eyes. Her eyes were glacial blue and held wisdom far beyond her youthful appearance. Her expression was one of anger and distaste for the entity standing before her.

The dark angel that stood before her matched her for size, but the face was pure evil and in its eyes a hatred that must have been there since its beginning.

"Demicides, who let you out of your prison? Lucifer must be desperate to have sent you here. He was certainly scraping the bottom of the barrel when he sent you. I'm surprised you would even attempt to take me on, but then I don't think he gave you any choice, did he?"

"Same old Auriel, always the bitch!" he growled.

She threw back her head and laughed at him. "Stupid demon, do you think you can really take me on and come out the winner? Don't you remember what happened the last time you challenged me? You cannot win, and you know it. Lucifer sends you to do his dirty work. He will sacrifice you so that he might get rid of the both of us at the same time."

"I have no choice in the matter; I will not return to be entombed again." He shouted lunging at Auriel.

They struggled together for what seemed like an eternity as Gabe watched. Two powerful beings locked together in combat. Every time one of them landed a blow the house, and everything around it shook with the force of it.

They wrestled together landing the occasional blow. The dark angel was powerful and deceptive. Breaking away from Auriel, he lunged at her again managing to wrap his hands around her throat. In the next moment, she broke his hold and shoved him away.

Trying to distract her he began squeezing Gabe's heart and cutting off his air supply. Gabe could feel himself losing consciousness.

Auriel knew he was trying to kill Gabe and at the same time draw her attention away from him. "Oh, no you don't, you will harm no one!" she said sending a burst of energy into Gabe to counteract what the demon was doing. Once that was done she sent another more powerful burst of energy at the demon sending it staggering back. It soon recovered and attacked her again. She struggled with it for several minutes than with a renewed surge of energy she created her flaming sword and held it to the demon's throat. It stopped struggling and started calling her all manner of names making wild threats against her and Gabe.

"Enough!" she told it, and the sound of her voice reverberated on both planes sending a shock wave through heaven itself. "As I see it you have one of three choices: entombment, I send you back to Lucifer or death. I actually prefer the third one, so which is it to be?"

Knowing what Lucifer would do to him if he were sent back and since he didn't want to die there was only one choice. "Entombment." He said reluctantly.

"A wise decision. I would say it's the lesser of the three evils, no pun intended." She said laughing.

Demicides winced at her words but knew he was far better off there than either of the alternatives.

"Michael, Gabriel, I think this one needs a spot far away from any living creature."

"I would have to agree with you, and I think we have just the place," Michael said.

"I know what you're thinking Michael, and I agree the spot you picked out is perfect. Shall we?" Gabriel asked.

"Yes," Michael said. Each grabbed an arm of the demon and disappeared.

Auriel could feel the lesser demon and its minions somewhere close by waiting for her to leave. "I summon you, followers of Lucifer in the name of Jesus Christ!" she shouted.

The lesser demon and his two minions were pulled against their will inside the house and stood before Auriel.

"You," she said pointing to the lesser demon, "were the one who planned this trap. What do you have to say for yourself?"

"I was forced to do it." He whined at her.

"You may have been under Democides control in getting me here, but you and you alone were responsible for terrorizing this family!" she said her eyes blazing.

"I will not apologize for it; these mortals deserve everything they get. Besides I enjoy making their lives a living hell!" He told her with relish.

"You have been on the earth plane too long. You were willing to sacrifice Demicides to save your skin."

"Hey, he had planned all along to do the same to me!" he shouted angrily at her.

"*SILENCE!*" She shouted, her voice shaking the walls of the house. "It's time you returned to the darkness where you belong and your minions with you! Gabriel, you are needed."

Gabriel appeared standing behind the demons. In one graceful movement, he enfolded them in his wings and disappeared.

As they disappeared, Auriel merged back into her physical body.

Sara felt utterly and completely exhausted. She was so exhausted that she was shaking visibly, she collapsed into the nearest chair and let out a sigh of relief. She closed her eyes and put her head back. She vaguely heard Gabe ask her a question but was unable to make out the words.

Sayetta appeared beside Sara and laid her hand on her head for a moment. She looked at Gabe and motioned for him to step outside. He left the house, and she followed silently behind him. "It will take her a few minutes to regain her strength. How are you feeling? You took a couple of good impacts to the chest."

"I'll be sore tomorrow but other than that I'll be fine." He said. "I've never seen or felt anything like that before."

"This type of thing does not happen often, but when it does, it is a sight to behold," Sayetta told him. "It's not every day you see an epic battle between good and evil. Are you still willing to go with me on this journey?" She grinned at him.

"Yeah, you can say that again. I feel that it's important for me to continue the journey with you. I'm not going to let one demon keep me from documenting these encounters or from doing the creators work." He told her earnestly.

"Good, then it's settled." She said smiling at him.

They heard the front door of the house open, and Sara appeared in the opening. She walked out to where they stood and asked Gabe, "Can you sage the house? I'll lay down the black salt after you finish." She texts the owners of the house that it was now safe to return.

"Sure, give me a minute to gather my equipment, and I'll get it done," Gabe told her heading inside the house.

"How is he?" Sara asked Sayetta.

"He'll be fine, a little sore tomorrow but otherwise he's okay. How are you feeling now?"

"I'm exhausted, but I'll manage. That's the first time Auriel has left my body completely; it was strange and terrifying at the same time. I'm not sure I want to repeat it again." She told Sayetta.

"I understand, and since it's not likely to happen again, I wouldn't worry about it. She only needed to come out to draw the attention away from the physical body. She didn't want it to kill the physical body so she stepped forward to confront it before it could do anything else. By the way, you passed your test." Sayetta told her.

"Well I'm glad to know it's not likely to happen again but if it does, then I'll be prepared." She told her. Heading back into the house, she found Gabe finishing the smudging.

"Well, that's done. Now, all we have to do is pick up the equipment, and we're out of here."

"Yes, the family should be home anytime, I text them to let them know we're finished." She told him.

They stepped outside just as the family pulled up in the driveway. Sara introduced Gabe and Sayetta then handed the woman the door key and told her, "Everything's gone now, you won't be having any more problems with anything attacking you or your children." Handing her a container of black salt she gave her instructions for laying it down. "This needs to be done now, do not wait." She instructed her.

"Don't worry we're going to do it as soon as you leave." The woman assured her.

Climbing into the car Gabe, Sayetta and Sara headed back to her house.

Looking at his watch, Gabe was surprised to see that barely an hour had passed since they arrived at the family's house. It seemed like they had been there for several hours. He'd be glad to get back to Sara's place so he could relax. He could tell that the battle had taken a toll on Sara and he hoped she would take a few days to relax.

About forty minutes later they arrived at the house. Gathering their things, they entered the house to be greeted by all five dogs.

"I don't know about the rest of you, but I'm going to take a nap before dinner," Sara told them.

"I agree I think I'll take one too," Gabe said heading towards the bedroom. Titus and Lucy followed him and climbed into their beds, Gabe laid down on his bed and was fast asleep.

With both of them sleeping Sayetta made her way up to the meditation room. Standing in the middle of the vortex, she connected with the creator. "Father, I have found and completed the quest for the first archangel, and she is on the right track. Do you have the location of the next Archangel for me?"

"Child, you will find the next one in England. You will receive further information as you did this time, the closer you get to the appointed time."

"Yes, father I understand."

Leaving the vortex, she went in search of a glass of iced tea. Entering the kitchen, she found Gabriel waiting; she was glad to see him.

"So, its England I hear." He commented.

"Yes, but not yet. I need more information: where in England and who am, I looking for. You wouldn't happen to know anything about it would you?" she asked him.

He grinned at her and commented, "You know better than that, it's a need to know basis and I don't need to know. Don't bother asking Michael either because neither one of us is privy to that information. Although I have heard through the grapevine that it's a male and he lives in London."

"Well, that's better than nothing I guess." She said smiling ruefully at him as he disappeared.

She spent the next two hours playing with the dogs and enjoying the farm animals. When she got back to the house, both Gabe and Sara were awake and were preparing dinner.

After dinner, they went into the living room and spent the next hour talking about the events of the day.

"Sara, I want you to know that you will feel an increase in your abilities in the next day or two. We will be leaving tomorrow morning to head back to Gabe's place in Arizona. We have a new assignment but don't know when we need to leave yet. All I do know is that we need to go to London, England."

"Well, I enjoyed having you both here and helping me through this ordeal." Looking at Gabe, she told him. "You need to keep in touch and keep me updated on your quest for the others."

"Don't worry I'll keep in touch and when I get back, you'll have to bring the dogs and come down and spend some time at the ranch." He told her sincerely.

"I think I would like that. If you need any help when you're in England just give me a shout and I'll hop a plane and be there in no time." She hoped that he would call, she looked forward to seeing him again.

"Don't worry if I need your help I won't hesitate to give you a call." He told her smiling. He would very much like to see her again. He was definitely attracted to her.

They left early the next morning and arrived back at the ranch three days later. About a week and a half after their return Gabriel showed up with a message.

Gabe was out feeding the animals when he felt someone standing behind him. Turning he saw Gabriel leaning against the barn door, his arms were folded over his chest and he had a funny look on his face.

"It's time." He said.

"Now?" Gabe asked.

"You leave in five days for London. There you will have to help him escape the darkness."

"Who will have to escape from the darkness? Does Sayetta know about this?"

"She does now." He told her disappearing.

"Five days" he muttered to himself, "talk about short notice!"

About the Author

June Lundgren is a psychic, medium, nurse, demon seer, animal communicator and international author. She is descended from a long line of Irish, Scottish and American Indian women with psychic and spiritual gifts. As a young child, she communicated with animals and angels.

She joined the military where she trained as a nurse and EMT. After returning from the military she continued to work as a nurse. She has been helping people with their animal issues, paranormal problems and giving intuitive readings. She was given the ability to remove negative entities twenty years ago, and has been quietly doing so since then.

Her first book, A Mediums Guide to the Paranormal, was released in 2009. Since then she has written 7 more books. She is an active member of Northwest Paranormal Investigative Team as an occult specialist on the team.

She loves working and helping animals and donates her animal communication abilities to local rescue groups.

Book website: www.demonseekers.com

My website: www.mysticconnections.org

For help with negatives, visit: **www.demonseer.com**

Connect with me on Twitter, Facebook, Pinterest, LinkedIn and Instagram